Emmet and the Boy

6-8-19

Emmet
and the
Boy

TERENCE O'LEARY

Swan
Creek
Press

ALSO BY TERENCE O'LEARY

Irish Crossings – Danny's Story

Irish Crossings – Caitlin & Paddy's Story

Bringing Boomer Home

Penalty Kick

More Than a Game

Swan
Creek
⮜Press

This book is a work of fiction. Names, characters, places and incidents either are products of the author's imagination or are used fictitiously. Any resemblance to actual events or locales or persons, living or dead, is entirely coincidental.

First Swan Creek Press, LLC Edition 2019
ISBN: 978-1-7335341-0-9
Library of Congress Control Number: 2018967871

www.terenceoleary.com

Design: Heather McIntyre, Cover&Layout |
www.coverandlayout.com
Cover Photo © Alessandro Cancian

For my Children

A teenager is just a grown boy
with a child's heart

Emmet and the Boy

CHAPTER 1

It was our time of the evening. I sat on the Adirondack chair at the water's edge. Warm water lapped my toes. Mia sat curled in my lap. Her bony hip pressed my stomach. The cancer had stolen her weight. She drifted between sleep and wakefulness. I wondered if she could feel my heart beating against her chest.

Her chair, where she usually sat, was empty beside us. The high-pitched whine of the Jet Skis faded, but the mosquitoes had yet to find us. This was the time we usually talked and reminisced in the evening's gloaming.

Weakening sunlight danced across the tips of shallow whitecaps. Across the lake, trees stood at the water's edge, their branches full and heavy.

Her body tightened. I held her gently until the spasm passed.

She said in a weak voice not more than a whisper, "You promised."

It took me awhile to answer, "It was such a long time ago."

Her cheek nestled my chest. I was glad I couldn't see her face. Her hand found mine and squeezed.

"You promised." Her words seemed filled with pain – or was it anger?

"Mia." I couldn't go on. My heart raced and the panic came.

She shuddered. The spasm was longer and harder. Her pain overcame mine. It took all my strength, but I stood. She weighed no more than a child. I gazed upon the lake that we so loved. The sand was firm beneath my feet. Mia was warm in my arms.

She gasped. Her frail body tightened. I backed away from the water. We walked the pebble path to the cottage not side by side, but with Mia in my arms.

Years ago we had screened in the porch. The breeze came off the lake. There was no need for the ceiling fan tonight. The furniture had been moved to the side to make room for the hospital bed. It was one of our arguments. I wanted the bed to be in our bedroom. She wanted the porch. I told her it was too hot during the summer afternoons, but she said, "Heat is my friend." It was another argument that I didn't win. At night I'd sleep on the cot beside her.

I guided the straw to her. It seemed to take all of her effort to swallow. When she finished, I took the ointment from the bedside table and coated her lips. The spasm came hard. By rote, my hand found the bag of syringes. I quickly tore one open and filled it with morphine. I didn't have to search for a vein. They put an intravenous therapy into her arm before we left the hospital. All I had to do was to insert the needle into the iv. The medicine took hold and Mia drifted to sleep.

I tried to read, but I couldn't. I set the book on the floor and turned off the reading lamp. Light from the cottage shined through the porch's window onto my wife. She lay on her back with her hands by her sides. It was strange, but when I looked at her, I saw the girl I married and not the woman she has become.

I walked to the screen and stared at the lake. The moon was full. Her summer midnight moon, she would say. I pictured her standing at the edge of the wooden slats leading out into the water. She'd shed what few clothes she wore and stand naked in the moonlight. She didn't care who saw her. Her buttocks were like two tiny white moons. She'd dive into the lake. I'd bring a towel for her and sit on the edge of the pier. When she tired, she'd swim to me like an enchanting mermaid. She'd climb up from the water and I'd wrap the towel around her and carry her to our bed.

The change in her breathing shook me from my reverie. I knew the morphine was wearing off. I sat by her side and held her hand. She must still be dreaming because her eyes danced beneath her eyelids. I wondered what she dreamed.

Her eyes opened. She stared at the ceiling. She seemed confused, trapped between dreams and wakefulness. I brought her hand to my cheek. She slowly turned and when our eyes met, all I saw was sorrow. It took me awhile to realize her face was reflecting mine.

She wet her lips and said, "You promised."

I let go of her hand and reached for the water cup. I brought the straw to her mouth, but like a little child, she shook her head. The spasm came sudden and hard. I prepped the morphine. Her pain brought tears to her eyes and to mine. She relaxed as the medicine took hold.

I sank back in the chair under the weight of an unbearable promise. The vials of morphine were waiting on the table. I held her hand as the hours passed. She stirred, but before she could awaken, I reached for the morphine.

Dawn came slowly and quietly. My only love lay as still as the calm water of the lake.

CHAPTER 2

The hospice nurse would come between 9 and 10 every morning. I had left the door unlocked. She knocked. When I didn't answer, I heard the door open. She called my name. Her footsteps echoed along the kitchen's wooden floor.

She stopped in the doorway. Her gaze went from Mia to me. She slowly walked to my wife. She checked Mia's vitals, but we both knew there was no need. She adjusted Mia's pillow as if that somehow would make her more comfortable.

She turned to me and asked, "Have you slept at all, Emmet?"

I shook my head.

"I need to make a phone call and then I can make some coffee."

I nodded. I looked upon Mia. Her hand was cold beneath mine. I knew her spirit was gone. I felt it leave during the night.

I seemed to be losing track of time. The nurse put the coffee cup in my hand.

"Do you want me to call your daughter?"

I knew it was my call to make, but I also knew my daughter. I simply nodded.

As the numbness left me, I tried to gather my thoughts. There were things that had to be done. Mia had made most of the decisions in the prior weeks. She said, if it was back in the time when we were both still teaching, she would want a service at the funeral home in the city. Our lives in many ways revolved around the high school, the students, and our fellow teachers. But it had been five years since we left Springfield High School. We'd kept in touch with just of few of our friends from our school days.

Our family was small. Both our parents were dead and both of us were only children. There was our daughter, Jackie, and our grandson, Colin. There were the neighbors, of course. They all knew of Mia's illness. Mia thought there was no need for a funeral service in the city. A small gathering at our cottage would do.

The nurse said the funeral director was on his way for Mia. He knew what she wanted. Together we would go with him. It was another promise that we made to each other a long time ago. The first to pass would witness the cremation of the other.

Jackie and Colin wouldn't get here until tomorrow. I would go with the funeral director. Mia couldn't wait that long.

CHAPTER 3

I stood on the dock and gazed upon our lake. There was enough light to see the still water, but not the trees on the far shore. I had to swim. The lake was empty except for a few early morning fishermen. Cottages along the bank were dark and silent. I wore my swimsuit and my rash guard. The white, long-sleeve shirt was easy to see in the water. It was another promise I made to Mia.

When I was younger, I used to swim across the lake, but those days stopped when I almost lost my life to a Jet Ski. Now, I swim in the predawn before the Jet Skis are allowed on the water. I hug the shore and swim where it is just deep enough for my arms to clear the bottom. No matter the weather, from late spring to early fall, I'd swim to the abandoned train trestle and back. It was part of my life.

Today, more than ever, I needed the familiar routine. I climbed down the ladder. In May the cold slap of water would make me gasp. Now, in August, it was like stepping into a warm bath. I didn't realize how tense I was until my muscles relaxed. I found my rhythm. My breaths came easy. I pushed all thoughts away and let the water cocoon me.

It takes an hour to swim to the trestle and back. During that hour the lake awakens.

I finished my swim. My arms were sore. My mind felt like it had been shut off and needed to be restarted. I treaded water by our dock. I took off my goggles, spit in them, and wiped them with my finger. When I swam near shore, I couldn't tell if my goggles fogged or if the water was sandy and cloudy with algae.

I checked the lake for boats and then swam to deeper water. I took deep breaths and dived beneath the surface. It was always a shock when I left the warm top layer of water and swam to the cold bottom. Away from the beach, the water was always clear. I ran my hand through seaweed that clung to the bottom of the lake. You couldn't see them from the surface, but small Bass blended with the green weeds. The pain in my lungs forced me to leave. I broke the surface and swam to the dock.

At first glance, I thought she was Mia. My daughter stood at the edge of the dock with her arms held tight across her chest. I climbed the ladder. The sun was behind her. She looked so like her mother.

"Dad! What are you doing? You scared me half to death."

She bent and grabbed my arm and helped me stand.

"I've been looking all over for you."

"You know I swim in the morning."

She shook her head in disbelief. "Mom just died and you're out swimming."

"It's what I do."

Jackie took my arms and shook me.

"Why didn't you wait? You could have waited a day."
Angry tears coated her cheeks. "I needed to say goodbye."

She pushed me away. She turned and fled down the
pier.

I took my swim shirt off and walked to the cottage. The
humid, early morning lake air clung to me like a second
skin. I pictured Mia sitting on the porch with her morning
coffee cup clutched between both hands. She'd wait for
me to finish my swim before our day together began.

I can't describe the loss that I felt. I'll never see my
Mia again. At times like this I wish I had religion and
could believe that we would meet again in the afterlife.

I climbed the porch's steps and opened the door. Mia
wasn't sitting in her chair. The boy sat in her place.

CHAPTER 4

Colin's head was buried in his iPad. He didn't notice my entrance. His fingers moved so quickly that I could hardly see them. He changed since I last saw him the past Christmas. He was in that pudgy stage of adolescence. His brown hair covered his ears and curled in around his neck. His face was oval like Mia's. He had soft androgynous features.

I slowly approached him and set my hand on his shoulder. He startled. His eyes darted to mine. He had my blue eyes. I gently squeezed his shoulder. I didn't really know my grandson. Mia and I would fly to California once a year to visit, but Jackie would draw us into her self-encompassing whirlwind and Colin would fade in the background.

"Do you have a password?" His voice was melodic. Something you would hear in a boys' choir. "You do have internet?"

His first words to me took me by surprise, but then he was Jackie's child.

"We do have internet. I'll have to look up the password. I wrote it down somewhere."

His iPad beeped. He returned to his game. I stood there feeling as if we lived in two different worlds.

I left him to his game and walked inside the cottage to the fireplace. Mia's ashes were in a simple box on top of the mantle. She didn't want an urn. She said there was no need. The box was biodegradable. She wanted to rest at the bottom of the lake. As the box diminished, her ashes would be freed to swim in the lake that she so loved.

"Why, Dad? Why couldn't you wait?" Jackie's angry voice came from behind me.

One of Mia's favorite photos was next to her ashes. I lifted the photo and stared at it. We were so young then. It was taken on one of our earlier trips to Paris. Mia asked a stranger to take the picture. We were on the Eiffel Tower with the city behind us. Mia always said it was a magical photo that captured a time that she would always treasure.

"Your mother wanted you and Colin to remember her the way she was. She didn't want your last memories to be a death bed photo."

I set the photo on the mantle and turned to my daughter. "Can you understand that, Jackie?"

Jackie bit her lower lip. Her eyes brimmed with tears. "I needed to say goodbye."

She stormed away from me. She went to the guestroom – her old bedroom – and slammed the door.

I felt Colin's eyes, but when I glanced to the porch, he was playing his game.

Chapter 5

There was no formal invitation. Word spread from one cottage to the next. The neighbors came and with them came the food. They came in the afternoon and talked in hushed voices throughout the cottage and on the porch. Mia would have liked it. They were old and dear friends.

Jackie was the hostess. Many of our neighbors could remember her as the little girl with ponytails who played hopscotch on the dock. Jackie was well suited for her role. She had arranged Mia's photo albums on the kitchen table. She sat with our neighbors gathered around her.

I don't know where the boy was.

Our next-door neighbors, the Petersons, had a pontoon boat that they docked on their side of the pier, which jutted out from our adjacent properties. We had a boat at one time, but when it came time to overhaul the engine, we decided we'd rather take a trip to Europe. We sold the boat and didn't miss it. We rarely used it. We're kayak people. We'd much rather glide silently across the lake under our own power.

John Peterson would captain the boat for Mia's last trip.

Mia wanted the evening. As the sun set behind the trees, she wanted her ashes to be returned to the sea. The pontoon boat wasn't big enough for all of us, but it didn't matter. We weren't going that far.

I carried Mia onto the boat and sat in the bow. Jackie took Colin's arm and led him onto the boat. She sat by me and Colin sat by his mother. John cast off and slowly steered the pontoon to a spot about 100 yards offshore. He dropped anchor. Our neighbors stood on the pier. They watched us and waited. There was a slight evening breeze and the boat gently rocked. It took me a long time to stand. The box was small and light in my hands, but the burden was so heavy.

John opened the gate in the railing and stood aside. I walked to the edge of the boat with Mia in my hands. I stood and stared at the water. I couldn't do it. I couldn't just drop Mia into the lake, never to know where she rested. Jackie came and stood beside me.

I held the box out to her.

Jackie didn't know what to do. I could tell she didn't want to hold her mother's remains. She finally extended her hands and reluctantly took the ashes.

I took off my shirt and slipped off my sandals. I stepped off the boat. Warm water engulfed me. I surfaced. I held the boat with one hand. I held my other hand out to Jackie.

Jackie knelt and set the ashes in my palm. I brought Mia to my chest. I pushed away from the boat and treaded water. I took deep breaths one after another and then forced the air from my lungs. I brought both hands around my wife. I drew a deep breath, tucked, and dived. I kicked and kicked. Mia's little weight seemed to help pull me downward. It was hard to see without my goggles, but as I got closer to the bottom, I saw a small opening between the seaweed.

I didn't want to let her go. I wanted to stay with my Mia. My lungs were on fire. The pain became too much. I gently released Mia to the sand. I swam to the surface.

I treaded water and looked to the shore. Our neighbors were still on the dock. I searched for landmarks. I needed to remember this spot.

Jackie knelt on the edge of the boat. I couldn't tell if her face was full of relief or sorrow. The boy stood behind her.

CHAPTER 6

It was a cloudy morning. There was no wind and ethereal mist hovered over the lake. I finished my swim. Jackie sat on the edge of the dock. I climbed the ladder. I glanced at my daughter and thought, what now? She worried her lower lip as she always did when she had something she didn't want to talk about.

Mia was my daughter's confident. When things were going well and Jackie was happy, we hardly ever heard from her. When she was troubled, she and her mother would spend hours on the phone. Jackie would often forget the time difference and call when we were asleep. Mia would get up and walk to the kitchen. She'd brew a cup of coffee as she listened to our daughter's rant.

Mia was our go-between. I learned of Jackie's divorce from her. I couldn't understand how two young people who were once so in love could end up hating each other. All I know is Jackie's husband left her for another woman. He abandoned her and his son. It's been two long years. I knew the scars my daughter carried. I wondered about the boy.

"Should we get a cup of coffee?" I asked.

"Can we talk here, Dad?" She tapped the dock.

I sat beside her. Our feet dangled over the edge. We both stared out at the water. I so wished Mia was here in my place.

Her words came out in a rush. "I've been seeing someone." She stopped and drew a breath.

"Does this someone have a name?"

"Darrell. Darrell Franklin." She paused. "We want to go to Europe together for two weeks."

She fell silent. I could feel her eyes upon me.

When I looked at her, she said with an intensity that scared me, "I need this, Dad."

"Then go."

She said so softly that it was hard to hear, "I want to leave Colin with you while I'm gone."

I don't know what she saw in my face.

She took my hand. "Please, Dad. It'll be good for you and for Colin. You shouldn't be alone right now."

Now, I knew why she didn't want to talk in the cottage. Her hand was shaking on mine. I could feel how anxious she was.

"I don't know if I can."

She pulled her hand from mine. Her voice hardened and the little girl who always got her way emerged. "I'm going with Darrell. If you can't watch Colin, I'll send him to camp." She didn't wait for an answer. She quickly stood and stomped to the cottage.

The sun came out and burned the mist away above the spot were Mia rested. If she were here, Mia would tell me that I had no choice. The boy was my grandson. My blood flowed in his veins. He came from me, but he also came from Mia.

CHAPTER 7

She had won. The happy child came out and chased the angry one away. Jackie morphed into the role of a loving daughter. She became over solicitous to both me and the boy.

We all sat at the kitchen table. Jackie painted a picture of an idyllic two week vacation for Colin. As she talked, she would glance at the Fitbit on her wrist to check the time. Colin rested his hands on top of his silent iPad. My daughter wove stories that were highlights of her teenage summers by the lake.

It was time. Jackie stood and then bent and hugged her child. She kissed his forehead. The boy sat rigid with his hands on top of his iPad. She stepped away from Colin. She leaned over and hugged me. She was my child. I hugged her back.

She moved away from the table and beamed as if she was already in Europe. She walked to the doorway and then glanced at her son. Colin had already turned on his iPad. She left without another word. I waited until I heard the rental car pull away from the house. I left the boy to his game. I stood and walked out to the lake.

Our two chairs were by the lake's edge. I walked and slowly sank into my chair. Mia's chair was empty. There was no hand to touch. I felt drained and hollow. It was too much. I didn't have the will to take care of myself. How could I take care of the boy?

The lake was coming alive. I could hear the angry whine of distant Jet Skis.

CHAPTER 8

"I'm hungry."

I don't know how long I sat or where my mind wandered. The boy stood in front of me. His ever-present iPad was by his side. I looked at him, but he averted his eyes. I tried to get my mind to think. I knew there had to be leftover food that the neighbors had brought.

"We'll find something for you."

I pushed up from my chair and led him to the cottage. Inside the refrigerator were leftover cold cuts and cheese. I pointed to the cupboard.

"Get yourself a plate."

I set the meat and cheese on the table. I took a loaf of bread from the breadbox that sat on the counter and slid it in front of him.

Colin sat and built himself a sandwich.

"Do you have any chips?"

I went to the cupboard and pulled out some Fritos. He took the bag from me, opened it, and poured the chips on his plate.

"We don't drink pop. I have coffee or milk."

"Milk works."

I poured a glass. I set it on the table and sat across from him. He turned on his iPad. One hand held his sandwich, the other played his game. He quickly became immersed in the game he was playing.

I felt like I had him for a few minutes, but now that his needs were filled, he was gone.

CHAPTER 9

August is a volatile month in Michigan. Heat builds during the day. Clouds form and sometimes thunderstorms follow. Our tranquil lake can quickly turn into a maelstrom.

I pulled our two kayaks further up on the shore and turned them over so that they wouldn't fill with water. I made it into the porch a few seconds before the dark clouds burst. Rain pelted the roof. I felt the hair on my arm rise. A fork of intense white hit the water beyond the pier. The flash of lightning was blinding. The following boom shook the windows.

The boy ran from the kitchen onto the porch. His face was white as the lightning. He had the look of a deer that didn't know whether to run or hide.

"It's OK, Col...."

Another flash lit the porch like daylight. The thunderous boom drowned my words. Lights flickered in the kitchen and then went out. A cool sudden gust of wind sheared through the screens. It felt like the temperature dropped 10 degrees.

Colin pushed his bangs back from his eyes. "What should we do?"

There was another flash of lightning. This time there were seconds before the boom.

"The storm's moving on. The worst is over."

I moved closer to the screen and looked out to the lake. The rain was steady, but not a downpour.

"I hoped the boats got off the lake in time."

Colin joined me by the year-round screens.

"Last year a small fishing boat got caught in a sudden squall. The boat was swamped and then capsized. Luckily, the two boys were close enough to shore and they were good swimmers."

Colin asked, "Has anyone ever died?"

"There have been a few deaths over the years, mainly from stupidity. City folks come out on the weekends. They don't know the lake. They don't know how to watch for weather or sandbars." I felt the bitterness enter my voice. "And then there are the Jet Skis."

We stood there and watched the sky brightening. It was still raining, but not a heavy downpour.

"Come on. Let's see what damage has been done."

I walked out from the porch and held the door open for the boy.

"It's raining," he said.

"It is."

The boy didn't know what to do. Maybe he thought I was a crazy old man.

"I promise you won't melt."

My words brought forth a rare smile. Colin followed me out into the rain.

I walked toward the pier and turned and looked at

the roof. There were tree branches on the roof, but no big limbs.

"It's warm," Colin said in surprise. "I thought rain would be cold." His damp T-shirt clung to his shoulders. Raindrops glistened on his cheeks.

I smiled and then turned and walked to the pier. "Look." I motioned across the lake. "The storm took one of the old ones." I pointed to a large tree that had fallen into the shallow water at the lake's edge.

The boy nodded. He lifted his bare arm up in front of his chest and watched rain bead on his skin. He had such a look of boyish wonder on his face.

CHAPTER 10

"How long will the power be out?"

The boy seemed distraught. He had changed into dry clothes, but his hair was still wet from the rain. He glanced down at his iPad. He reminded me so of his mother when she would get upset.

"I don't know, Colin. It all depends. It can be minutes or hours. One time it didn't come back on for two days."

"Do you have a portable charger?"

"What's that?"

He shook his head in frustration. "It's a small, little … it's like a battery. You plug your iPad into it when there's no power. Damn." He shook his iPad and for a second, I thought he was going to throw it to the ground. I don't know if he said to me or to himself, "Mom must have taken mine."

"It's not the end of the world, Colin."

He glared at me. He had his mother's temper. I did what I would do with my daughter. I just walked away.

I went to the kitchen. Even with the power off, evening light coming through the windows illuminated the room. Dishes were piled in the sink and the garbage can was overflowing. Our photo albums were still on the table. First things first, I would put the albums away. One of the albums was still open. I went to close it, but I was drawn to the photos. I sat at the table and let the memories return.

I felt the boy's presence. He stood in the doorway.

"Come here."

I moved the adjoining chair back from the table and he slid into it. The photo album was between us.

"It might be hard for you to believe, but your grandma and I were young once. These photos go back to a time before your mother was born."

I rested my finger next to Mia's photo. It hit me all at once. My throat closed. I tried to swallow, but I couldn't. The thought that I would never see her again, never touch her, never hear her voice. I turned away from the boy. I felt paralyzed in the awkward silence.

The lights came on. The refrigerator hummed. I heard the scuff of his chair across the wooden floor and then his footsteps. I turned and looked back upon my Mia's photos.

Beeps came from the boy's game on his iPad in the other room.

CHAPTER 11

My morning swim was done. It was a beautiful day. One of the waning days of summer that held just a hint of fall in the air. The boy was missing it. He slept in my daughter's old bedroom. The door was closed. It was getting on to noon. I didn't know if I should worry, if I should go and check on him. I knew that sooner or later his hunger or his full bladder would drive him from his bed.

I sat on the porch and tried to read. I heard the toilet flush. I breathed a sigh of relief. He appeared in the doorway. His hair stuck up at odd angles. He wore the same clothes that he wore yesterday, cargo shorts and a T-shirt. His feet were bare and they seemed too large for the rest of his body. His iPad was by his side.

He came onto the porch and with him came the boy smell. It took me back to the high school where I taught for 40 years. The smell must have something to do with hormones. It's distinct and not pleasant.

"What do we have to eat?" he asked. Dried drool caked the corner of his mouth.

I stood and went to him. He was not as tall as me, but one day I knew he would be taller. His shoulders were round. He stood slightly stooped, as did most adolescents as if they weren't used to their extra height.

"Do you eat breakfast or lunch in the middle of the day?"

He looked at me quizzically. "I'm still on California time."

I managed a smile. "I forgot. Breakfast it is."

We went to the kitchen. He plopped down at the table and turned on his game.

"The cupboards are getting pretty bare. We'll have to go shopping." I opened the refrigerator. "I can scramble some eggs. You're not allergic?"

"No." Colin's head hovered over his iPad. His fingers danced.

I don't eat much, but then I'm not a growing boy. Colin devoured half a dozen scrambled eggs. I needed to get more food for the boy. Churchill's general store was closest. It was at the entrance of the only road that circled our lake. It survived for generations because it was close and people who needed just a few things would go there. Churchill's was expensive. If the lake visitors really wanted to stock up, they'd go right by Churchill's and drive out to the Walmart by the highway.

Colin sat at the table engrossed in his game. I could leave him at the cottage and drive to Churchill's, but that isn't what I wanted or what I thought he needed.

I opened the closet and took out the backpack.

"Colin." I set the backpack on the table.

"What's this," he asked.

"We're going shopping."

"With a backpack?"

"You'll thank me when you're carrying the food home. You'll need shoes. I'll give you a hat if you don't have one. And Colin, leave the iPad here."

CHAPTER 12

The boy didn't have a hat so I gave him one of my old Mud Hens baseball caps. He wore sneakers, but no socks. I grabbed a plastic bottle of bug spray from the cupboard and led him outside.

"Hands up," I said.

He dropped the backpack. He gave me a curious smile as he lifted his arms. I sprayed him, clothes and all.

"It stinks."

"That's why we don't put it on inside the cottage."

"Where are we going anyways?"

"We're going to Churchill's to get food to feed that bottomless pit you call a stomach. Just remember, whatever you get you have to carry home."

I sprayed myself and set the bug spray on the porch's steps. I picked up the backpack and tossed it to him. I turned and set off walking. I didn't look back, but I heard the boy's shuffle behind me.

Only old folks like me knew about the path. It was originally a deer path and then an Indian path that wandered along the lakeshore. When they built the newer cottages, the owners thought they owned the land going all the way down to the water. It didn't matter to me if they did or not. I still followed the path. Occasionally, an owner, especially a young one, would come out and confront me. I'd explain about the path. I think some of them thought I was just a crazy old man, but they all let me cross.

It was an easy walk along the shore between the lake and the cottages. Most people who saw me waved and I waved back. A few of them scowled. One mother, who saw me coming, chased her children inside.

We got to the last cottage. I stopped and waited for the boy to catch up with me.

"We have a decision to make. There are two ways to go up ahead. We can stay on the path. It goes down by the lake. It's good now. In spring we couldn't go that way because the ground's too swampy. That's why they can't build any cottages there."

I pointed to the hill rising from the lake. "Our other choice is to go up on the road. It would be an easier walk." I swept my hand back to the lake. "The path is a harder walk, but it's shorter and quicker. But I have to tell you it's narrow, just wide enough for a deer. You'll have to stay behind me. And there are bugs."

I studied him to see his reaction. I added to try and sway him, "I'm for taking the deer path."

The boy's cheeks were red. His forehead glistened with sweat under the baseball cap. His face remained blank.

"Are you up to this?"

He seemed surprised by the question and didn't

know how to answer.

I pointed back toward the way we came. "If you want you can go back to the cottage. I'll go to the store by myself."

"No. I'll go with you."

I was a bit surprised, but it was the answer I hoped for.

I asked, "We'll take the path?"

He hesitated and then reluctantly nodded.

"OK. But keep an eye out for snakes."

I laughed at his startled expression.

"Just kidding. We'll be fine."

I thought I saw a hint of a smile.

CHAPTER 13

The path was overgrown with vegetation. In some spots the foliage was as high as my shoulders. Beyond the undergrowth, trees stood like silent sentinels. Even in August, everything was still green and lush by the water. It was like being cocooned in Mother Nature's womb. Silence engulfed us. Gone were the sounds of cars on the road and boats on the lake.

But there was a price to pay. As the path moved closer to the lake there were patches of still water. Bugs were thick, especially mosquitoes and gnats. I heard the boy slap.

I turned to him. "Don't. That's why you have the bug spray. Just leave them alone. They'll hover, but they won't land on you."

My words were met with a look of a true skeptic. Colin took off his cap and tried to shoo the mosquitoes away. I shrugged and continued our journey.

The path forked. Even a novice could see that the main path went forward. I looked back at the boy and then chose the less traveled path that led down to the lake. I walked slowly and quietly. The boy followed my example. It was a true deer path and more than once, especially in the early morning, I've encountered a deer on his way back from watering at the lake. The path was wide enough for only one of us. I was the one who always chose to move off the path to let the deer pass. It was too late in the day. I didn't expect to see any deer, and I was right.

We left the mosquitoes behind. The path ended at a small opening by the lake. A tree trunk had washed ashore ages ago. Someone had pulled it up from the water. I went and sat. The log was wide enough for two. It was one of our favorite resting places. I glimpsed Mia sitting by me and then she was gone. The boy walked to the edge of the water and stared at the lake.

I wondered what he was thinking. I'd spent 40 years with teenagers, but don't ask me what they were thinking. It's the most secretive age. Even the ones who would take me in their confidence would hold back.

The boy looked my way. I scooted over to give him more room on the log. He came and sat heavily beside me. The armpits of his T-shirt were sweat stained. His damp bangs clung to his forehead beneath his Mud Hens cap. His cheeks were flushed. He had the whitest teeth.

"It's so quiet," he said.

"That's because the lake is shallow and narrow here. No motorboats or Jet Skis can navigate the water, only kayaks and canoes." I pointed. "See how close the far bank is and how the water flows. This tributary leads from our lake to the next."

"The next lake?"

"Michigan has over 11,000 inland lakes. Many of them are connected."

He pondered my words.

"There's a lot of history here. At one time this was all Indian land. I wouldn't be surprised if Indians sat on this very log."

He smiled and said, "You're kidding."

"This spot's here for a reason. Indians would get around by canoe. They'd see a deer by the water. They'd pull their canoes up here and follow the deer path. Just like the lakes, the deer paths are connected. The Native Americans would hunt for their dinner, bring it back here, and carry it home by canoe."

I looked at him asked, "Can you picture it?"

He tried to laugh my words away, but I kept my eyes upon him.

"You're not kidding."

I shook my head.

His gaze went slowly from the lake to our clearing to the deer path.

"They have guns or bows and arrows?"

"Bow and arrows and spears before the white man came. Sometimes they would even chase down a deer with just a knife."

His face scrunched in concentration. Silence lingered between us. He slowly nodded and said, "I can see it."

"There's so much to see, Colin, if only you would open your eyes and look."

He stared at me with a seriousness that belied his age. I wondered if I touched him.

I smiled and said, "We have our own hunting and gathering to do."

I stood too quickly. I wobbled. I put my hand on the boy's shoulder to steady myself as I waited for my blood flow to catch up to my brain. The dizziness passed.

Colin looked at me in alarm.

"It's nothing."

To prove it to myself and the boy, I extended my hand and when he took it, I helped him to his feet.

CHAPTER 14

If the lake had an historic landmark, it would be Churchill's. The building was built in the late 19th century and like all buildings of that time period it was built from the abundant forest. There was still a hitching post in front of the entrance. Occasionally, I'd still see a tethered horse.

Churchill's started and remained a general store. Whatever the weekend cottagers forgot to bring from home could be found at Churchill's. Electricity was a later addition and you could see the exposed wires running along the overhead oak beams. You won't find air conditioning, just open screen windows and large sweeping electric fans. Lighting was poor and dust abundant.

Food staples were on one side and hardware the other. In summer a side door led to an open covered annex. Tables and bins were filled with local fruits and vegetables that were picked that same morning. The owner had an uncanny knack to buy just enough so that by the end of the day the tables were bare. Mia would plan our summer meals around the harvest.

There was a time when the aisles were full. Especially in the morning, when the fresh bread and produce were brought out, you couldn't push a cart through the aisles without bumping into people. When Mia came here with me, she'd spend more time talking – what I'd call gossiping – than shopping.

The store, like the lake, had changed with the times. When I was younger, our lake was a family place. You'd find three generations under the same roof during summer vacations. Children who prospered would buy land next to their parents. They'd build their own cottages so that they could relive their idyllic childhood through the eyes of the next generation.

But that all changed in the last decade. Land speculators discovered our lake. New cottages sprang up at the start of every new season, but they weren't wood cabins. The new owners from the city wanted lake houses. They built sleek glass edifices that reflected the sun. The lake went from rowboats and canoes to power boats and Jet Skis.

The new owners brought with them their Walmart that was built down by the highway. They hardly ever shopped at Churchill's. For those who stopped, Churchill's was mainly a curiosity. The store was something to be talked and maybe laughed about over their evening meal.

Now, you don't have to worry about bumping into someone in the aisles. There were only a handful of people in the store. There were still enough locals who supported Churchill's, at least for now, to keep the store open, but I don't know about the future.

The boy had wandered off. I walked up to the meat counter. I had a limited repertoire to match my meager cooking skills. I could scramble eggs and make pancakes. My next step up was chicken and rice. I thought I could handle that for the boy and add some fresh vegetables.

The boy found me. He had half a dozen frozen packages of macaroni and cheese.

He dumped the boxes into the cart and said, "I know you have a microwave."

I asked in disbelief, "Where did you find those?"

He waved his hand in the direction of one of the aisles.

"Mom says she doesn't have time to cook. These aren't bad. They're easy to make. You just zap them in the microwave. I have them just about every day."

If Mia were here, she would have thrown a fit. She'd give him a lecture about healthy eating. She'd have the boy put the packaged food back. But she's not here. I looked at the boy. It was a fight I didn't want to have. Colin has his boy shrug. I did my old man shrug.

"Let's get some vegetables."

He countered, "How about some ice cream?"

"Are you going to run all the way home?"

It took him a second. "You're right. It'd melt. No ice cream."

CHAPTER 15

There were two men waiting behind the cottage when we returned on the path by the lake. They wore some sort of uniforms, but I didn't know what. I walked ahead of the boy.

The taller of the two asked as I approached, "Are you Mr. Hyland?"

"I am."

"Didn't you get my message? I left you a voice mail yesterday. We're here for the bed."

It took me awhile to understand what he was saying.

He softened his voice. "It's OK, Mr. Hyland. We'll just get the bed and be on our way."

I turned and motioned the boy to the porch. "Colin, go put the food away."

He walked around me. His shoulders were hunched forward to compensate for the weight of the backpack.

I asked, "Your truck's out front?"

"Yes, out by the road."

"It'll be easier to take the bed out from the back of the porch and walk it around the side of the cottage." I led them up the porch steps.

The hospice nurse had taken everything but the bed. The end table that held Mia's medicine stood empty. Jackie had stripped the sheets from the hospital bed. She washed the sheets and put them away.

My cot, where I slept beside my wife, was still by the hospital bed. My sheets and pillow were on the cot. I still slept there. I went and sat on the cot and stared at the empty bed. I didn't see my Mia. I refused to see her there.

It took me a minute to realize that the two men were still by the doorway.

I waved to the bed. "It's OK."

They quietly went about their business as I sat on the cot.

I didn't see them out. I sat until I heard the truck pull away. I knew I wasn't ready to return to our bedroom. I couldn't bear the thought of being in our bed by myself. I pushed the cot to the empty spot where the hospital bed had been. I would continue to sleep on the porch. It was cool out here in the evening and I was closer to the lake and my Mia.

I slipped off my sandals and lay on the cot. I couldn't bear the emptiness. I missed her voice. We were friends as much as lovers. Now, when I needed her most to talk with, she wasn't here.

I closed my eyes. I didn't know if I had the will to go on without her.

The beeps came from the kitchen. I knew the boy was at the table with his iPad.

CHAPTER 16

I spent my morning swim thinking about what I could do with the boy. I was counting the days down that he would be here. I was down to 10.

I found him sitting at the kitchen table eating cereal. I set my towel on the chair seat and sat across from him in my damp swimsuit.

"Do you know how to swim?"

The boy swallowed a mouthful of cereal. "My mom made me take swimming lessons when I was little. She said, 'If you live by the ocean, you have to know how to swim.'"

"If you live by the lake, you have to know how to swim."

The boy furrowed his eyebrows.

"It's what we always told your mother when she was little."

"So, I have you to blame."

I laughed. "You don't like swimming?"

"There are other things, I'd rather do."

"Like play your game?"

His face tensed and I knew I hit a nerve. He refilled his bowl with cereal and poured milk on top.

"We have a beach here. I'll admit it's not much of a beach. They just roped off one area of the lake to keep the boats and Jet Skis out. I'll take you down there this afternoon. It's always been a local hangout for teenagers. Maybe you'll meet someone your age."

It was written all over his face that he didn't want to go.

"We'll go together. If you don't like it, we'll just come back."

I have a car, but in summer, I hardly ever drive it. I'm not one of the old folks who get around in golf carts. I think they look ridiculous. We could kayak down to the beach, but I don't know if the boy was ready for that. That left walking, which was fine with me. I didn't ask the boy's opinion.

I said it was time to go. I expected the boy to say he had a stomach ache or give some other lame excuse so he could stay at the cottage, but he surprised me. He came out of his bedroom. He wore his swimsuit and a T-shirt with flip-flops. He stuffed two towels and his iPad into the backpack. I handed him the sunscreen and two plastic bottles of water. He wore the cap I gave him. I felt good about that.

The road circled the lake. It was barely wide enough for two cars to pass each other. The speed limit was 20, but hardly anyone went that fast. There were curves and potholes, hidden driveways and kids on bicycles.

We had hardly left our driveway when Colin asked, "How far is it?"

"Not far."

The boy rolled his eyes.

I kept walking and he followed. We rounded the bend and I stopped in my tracks. There was a dump truck in the Brennan yard. A crew of workmen was demolishing the cottage. I hated to see it.

"What are they doing?" Colin asked.

I wanted to go and yell at the workers. To shake my fist in their face and say, "There's no need to tear it down. There's nothing the matter with the cottage. It's been in the Brennan's family for over 100 years. They took good care of it."

Colin whined, "Why are they tearing it down?"

I couldn't keep the anger from my voice. "The parents are gone and the kids sold out. The property is worth much more than the cottage. They'll clear the land and next year you'll see a half-million-dollar house on the lake, and more Jet Skis on the water."

The boy seemed like he wanted to say something, but I think my anger made him swallow his words.

Chapter 17

I couldn't figure out why the beach was so crowded.

"What day is it?"

The boy gave me one of his looks like he didn't know if I was serious or kidding.

"It's Saturday."

"That explains it."

The boy shook his head. He moved a little farther away from me.

Now that I got him here, I didn't know what to do with him.

Colin seemed to know what to do. He sauntered away from me up to the tree line at the end of the sand. He walked into the shade of the trees. He slid his backpack off, took out his towel, and spread it on the sand. He took his iPad and sat Indian style with the game in his lap.

I went and stood next to him. He didn't take his eyes off his game. With one hand, he reached into the backpack and took out the other towel. He handed it to me. I spread it on the ground and sat by him.

He said, "If the weather's good, Mom drags me along to the beach on Sunday afternoons. She needs her sun time." He stretched his legs in front of him. "It doesn't matter to me; I can play my game anywhere." He looked up toward the sun. "The satellite is up there somewhere."

"Your mother…" I didn't know if I should say what I felt. "…If you stood in front of a mirror together, your mother would only see herself."

His fingers paused. I waited for the boy to respond. The iPad started to beep. His fingers moved.

I looked away from him to the beach. I tried to remember the last time we were here. It must have been when Jackie was little. We'd lay our towels close to the water, so we could keep an eye on Jackie as she tried to build sand castles with her tiny shovel and pail. It wouldn't be long before the little one became bored and frustrated. It was always Mia to the rescue. They'd work together and when finished with their castle, they'd frolic in the shallow water.

I could see them. Mia had the body of a dancer, thin and lithe. Her movements were fluid. Even at rest, my wife would look graceful. It was such a happy time in our lives. Her eyes would twinkle before the smile reached her lips.

She was a tease and I loved her for it. All it took was a coy glance and I would stop whatever I was doing and go to her.

The boy took a water bottle from the backpack. Mia disappeared. I glanced at him and wondered if something was the matter with his body chemistry. Even in the shade, he was dripping sweat.

"It's hot," I said. "Why don't we go cool off in the water?"

He studied the beach and seemed torn by indecision. I stood. "Come on."

He shoved his iPad into the backpack and then he covered the backpack with his towel.

I took off my cap and peeled off my T-shirt and tossed them on my towel. I waited for the boy to do the same. He stood and took off his cap. He looked furtively around at the other beach dwellers.

I had forgotten what it was like to be a young teenager. Even the best of them have poor self-images. I tried to image how Colin felt. I waited.

He slowly lifted and took off his T-shirt. His arms were tan but his chest was white as bleached flour. Like so many his age, he had that adolescent pudginess that came with puberty. His shoulder and arm muscles were undeveloped. Fatty tissues made his small breasts look almost like a girl's. I feared the taunts he would get in a high school locker room surrounded by his peers. Teenagers can be so cruel.

He stared at the ground and I wondered if it was shame that he felt.

"Hey." I waited until he looked up at me. I smiled and tried to make it seem like no big deal. "Let's go cool off."

I walked by his side down to the water.

CHAPTER 18

He surprised me. The boy could swim. He was graceful in the calm water of the lake. His technique was good. I had taught myself to swim. It wasn't until I was an adult and read books on swimming that I realized how many strokes I had been doing wrong. Colin knew the fundamentals.

We swam away from shore and stopped. We stood on the mushy bottom. The water was up to my shoulders and up to the boy's chin.

"I guess the lessons took," I said.

He sucked in a mouthful of water, then spit it in an arch back to the lake.

He gave me a challenging look and said, "My Mom must have done something right."

"You look at her as your mother. I look at her as my daughter. We don't see her from the same eyes."

He wasn't a quick one to respond. I don't know if that was good or bad. I knew that he pondered my words and when he was ready, he would reply.

I cocked my head to the deeper water. "See the rope?"

He used his hands and feet to kick up from the water. He searched and then fell back.

"I see it."

"I'll race you to it." I didn't wait for his answer. I tucked and swam.

I kept looking back. I wondered if I pushed him too hard. He wasn't in shape like me. To swim distance, you need to find a rhythm in the water and when you do, you can swim forever. The boy couldn't find his rhythm. I watched him struggle and then he floundered.

The water was deep. The lake's not like a swimming pool. When you get tired in the pool, you can swim to the edge and hold on. In the lake there's nothing to hold onto. I saw panic in his eyes. I swam to him as quickly as I could.

He thrashed the water and gulped air. I grabbed his shoulder and turned him toward me.

I shouted in his face, "Tread water!" I backed away from him. "Tread water!" I dog-paddled in front of him to demonstrate.

He quit thrashing. He let his feet drop. His hands and feet made quick circles in the water. His chest heaved as he struggled for air.

"You're OK, Colin. Relax. You're OK. I'm right here. I'm not going anywhere."

The wildness left his eyes. His gasps turned to deep breaths.

I treaded water and watched him calm.

"Lean back and float."

His feet came up and his hands went out to his sides.

His chest slowed. He waved his hands in the water and gently kicked his feet. I stayed beside him close enough to touch him. I tried to ignore the tightness in my chest.

"You're OK, Colin."

His breathing became slow and easy.

"You must learn, Colin. Don't fight the water. Become part of it."

He stared up at the sky. I wish I knew what he was thinking.

Chapter 19

We didn't talk on the way back to shore. When his feet could touch, he walked on the sand up to the beach. As he emerged from the water, he crossed his arms against his chest, as a shy girl would. He ignored the people on the beach. He went straight to his backpack. Even though he was still wet, he quickly slid on his T-shirt. He wiped his hands on the towel and grabbed his iPad. He sank down onto the sand.

I slowly followed him. I sat beside him and left him to his game. The tightness in my chest had eased. It wasn't the first time I had the pain and I knew it wouldn't be the last. The pain didn't scare me. I accepted it as part of growing old. What scared me was what would have happened if I couldn't help the boy. It was my own fault for pushing him into something that he wasn't ready to handle.

Maybe it would be better if I left him alone. Maybe he'd be safer staying in his own world with his game.

I looked out upon the beach. It had changed since I was young. There were still families with toddlers by the water. Middle-age couples sat in beach chairs and nursed their beers or plastic cups of wine. Missing were the teenagers. In my youth this was our gathering spot for our summer by the lake. The air would be filled with flying Frisbees. There was always an impromptu volleyball game in the sand. Teenage girls would lie on bright colored towels basking in the sun while working on their summer tans.

I had to drag Mia here. She was never a sun bunny. She said she didn't have the patience to lie in the sun and bake.

There are a few teenagers on the beach today, but not like before. Where are the rest? I know they're here at the lake. I see them in the store or walking the roadside. They're just not at the beach. Maybe they're all like Colin, hiding in their own fantasy world. Maybe the games were the new Pied Pipers leading all the teenagers away.

Chapter 20

The fire ring was near the water on the right side of our property away from the pier. It has always been part of my life at the cottage. Even on a warm summer evening, I would build a fire. I loved the smell of wood smoke and to sit and watch the flames dance.

A storm had taken one of our trees years ago. We cut up the trunk and used the pieces of logs as chairs. Rocks, turned black from the fire over decades, formed the ring. The fire's smoke kept the mosquitoes away. Mia and I would sit on our logs for hours and talk. Pauses in our conversation would come, but we didn't feel a need to fill them. We'd stare at the flickering flames, each lost in our own thoughts.

"This is a good place to talk, Colin."

The fire was between us. There wasn't any wind. Smoke drifted straight up to the dark sky. His iPad was in the cottage. I almost expected his fingers to start twitching. He sat and looked at me as if he didn't know what he was supposed to do.

"I lost track. How old are you?"

"Thirteen. My birthday's in May."

I had forgotten. Mia was the one who always sent the birthday cards and checks.

"Thirteen. You're going into high school?"

He nodded.

"How do you feel about that?"

He shrugged and I laughed.

"It takes a while to learn the fine art of conversation." I stood and picked up a piece of driftwood from a pile set off to the side. I tossed it on top of the fire.

I sat back down and rested my hands on my knees. "It's a big step going from junior high to high school. You go from the top being an eighth grader to the bottom being a freshman. I remember the first time I walked into my high school, I was scared. There were hundreds of strange teenagers and I only knew a few of them. I was small and they all seemed to tower over me. It was only when I made new friends that I found out that we were all scared. Part of being a freshman is being scared."

I waited for him to respond, but he just stared into the fire.

"In some ways it's good."

He looked up at me.

"Being scared, I mean. It means you're alive. Were you scared out on the lake?"

Even with the fire, I could see his cheeks blush.

"I panicked."

"That was my fault. I should have known better."

He did a shoulder shrug not accepting or denying what I said.

The boy got a dreamy look in his eyes. "Time slowed down. It was like everything was happening in slow motion."

"The mind does that in times of great stress. I don't know why."

"I knew how to tread water. Why didn't I?"

"You would have eventually."

"You think so?"

"The body has a strong desire to survive. Like you said, you know how to tread water."

He slowly shook his head and said quietly, "I don't know about the strong desire to survive."

I stared at him, but the boy seemed lost in the fire.

CHAPTER 21

I had a troubled morning swim. Usually, I just let my mind drift. I'd bounce from thought to thought as my body flowed in its natural rhythm through the water. This morning, the boy's words from the fire haunted me.

One thing I learned from over 40 years of teaching was that depression is part of every teenager's life. The root of it comes from disappointment; from never being able to live up to your own or others' expectations.

For some high schoolers, depression is too much. I've had a few students over the many years that I taught who committed suicide. Each one haunts me. I didn't see the signs. I don't know if I could have stopped them, but if I had known what they were going through, I could have tried to help.

I felt the boy was showing me signs, but teenagers are so secretive. How do I find out what he is going through?

I finished my swim. I stopped at the ladder. It was Sunday morning and the lake was still and quiet. I felt her calling me. I swam away from the dock. I didn't have to go far. I treaded water until I found my landmarks.

A cloud passed and sunlight rippled across the water. I hyperventilated, exhaled, and then tucked and dived. With my goggles, I could see sunrays shine upon the bottom of our lake.

I found my Mia nestled among the seaweed. The package was ragged. I don't know if it was natural deterioration or if the fish were pecking away. I knew it didn't matter to Mia. She was where she longed to be.

I swam to her and let my hand caress the package. I thought if only you were here to talk with.

I felt her quintessence floating in the water as if she was trying to touch me.

I don't know if the pain knifed my lungs or my heart, but it became too much. I had no choice. I broke to the surface and gasped for air. I treaded water until my heart calmed.

I sat in my Adirondack chair. Mia wasn't here to counsel me. I had no idea what I could do to help the boy.

Our lake was calm and tranquil and beautiful. This is where we had spent the happiest times of our lives. I closed my eyes. Water gently lapped against the shore. It was as if the lake had its own heartbeat. The sun and a soft morning breeze warmed and dried the moisture from my skin.

A morning like this was why we could never give up our cottage. A morning like this brought back all the happy times we shared together.

I had my memories. Mia would always live inside me. I could visit with her whenever I wanted to. It was easy to catch and relive the times we shared and cherished. I knew my Mia would never abandon me.

My thoughts turned to the boy. He had his life ahead of him and his own memories to be made. But how do I reach him?

CHAPTER 22

I surprised the boy. He sat at the kitchen table. The empty bowl and cereal box were pushed off to the side. He didn't have his iPad, but in his hands were one of the photo albums that I had yet to put away. He was concentrating so hard on the pictures that he didn't hear me enter until I opened the refrigerator. I took out a bottle of water. I grabbed a banana from the counter. I went and sat by him.

He looked at me with uncertainty. His hair was tousled from sleep. I don't know why his cheeks were flushed. His hands were on top of the photos as if he were trying to hide them. I gently pushed his hands off the album. I looked down at Mia and me. It hit me hard: the thought that I could never physically touch her again. To never feel the warmth of her embrace. But the feeling passed, replaced by memories of our time together.

I felt the boy's eyes. I looked at him. He was worrying his lower lip. He reminded me of his mother.

"It's OK, Colin." I opened the bottle and took a sip. I glanced back to the photos. "We didn't have the money to go to France, but we went anyway. Your grandmother knew she was pregnant. We had always talked about going to Paris. Mia said if we didn't go right away we may never go. So we threw caution to the wind and went."

I took another sip of water. The memories flowed from the photos. "We were there for a month. We spent two weeks in a small village in southern France. Mia practiced her French. We leisurely walked the cobblestone streets hand in hand. We'd have our morning coffee and croissants at an outside café. At night, we'd sleep on a feather bed. Mia would take my hand and put it on her stomach to feel the life growing inside her."

I took a breath. I would not tell the boy how Mia and I made love with a passion that only the young possess. Those memories were too personal to be shared.

I turned the page. "We spent the last two weeks in Paris. We were so young. Paris is an enchanting city. We fell under its spell. Of all the cities that I have visited, Paris is my favorite. If ever you find a girl that you truly love, you must take her to Paris."

I glanced at my grandson. "Or a boy."

I expected him to laugh, but his cheeks reddened with embarrassment.

I had forgotten what it was like to be a boy his age to have all those hormones running wild and crashing into each other, to be shy around girls, but comfortable around boys.

"Your body is changing so rapidly right now, Colin. You don't know what you want. It's OK to be confused. Give it time and it will settle. It doesn't matter if you like a girl or a boy. What matters is to find someone."

He wouldn't look at me as he said, "I'm not gay." I didn't understand his need for the denial.

"I'm not saying you are. You're missing the point. It doesn't matter to me if you are gay or straight. Life is about finding someone, Colin. We're not meant to live alone."

He snapped, "Tell that to my mother."

His anger took me by surprise. He had his mother's temper. The look in his eyes from someone so young froze me. I expected a re-enactment of one of Jackie's tantrums. His hands shook with anger.

I met his stare and waited.

He seethed. I felt his breath on my face. I braced for the coming storm.

The boy shook his head. He snatched his iPad from the table. He fled to his bedroom.

I sat at the table. I tried to understand what just happened. Even with the bedroom door closed, I could hear the beeps from his game on his iPad.

CHAPTER 23

I read for a while on the porch. The cottage was quiet, but the lake was alive. Pontoon boats glided like swans across the water. Jet Skis, like enemy fighter planes, buzzed around them. I knew I had to do something. I couldn't let him stew. I'd only have the boy for another week and then he would be gone.

I knocked on his bedroom door. I waited a few seconds and then knocked again.

He shouted, "What?"

I opened the door. He was lying on his bed, his head propped up with pillows. The iPad rested on his stomach.

"It's too nice of a day to spend inside. Get your swimsuit on."

His petulant voice answered, "I don't want to go swimming."

I used my teacher's voice. "We're not going swimming. Five minutes." I closed the door and left him to dress.

I dragged my kayak to the water's edge. I went back for Mia's kayak. I stood over the boat and stared at the empty seat. My heart fluttered. I sank down onto her kayak. I rested my hand where she sat for so many voyages. I looked to the water beyond the dock. I knew she was there, but sometimes I was overwhelmed with the feeling that she was still with me.

"Grandpa."

The voice brought me back. The boy stood in front of me. I didn't hear him come from the cottage. I wondered how long I had sat on Mia's kayak. He seemed worried. I was beginning to wonder if it was me that he was worried about. He wore his baseball cap and a baggy white T-shirt over his blue swimsuit.

"Is it waterproof?" I pointed to the iPad, which was beginning to seem like an extension of his hand.

He gave me a confused look.

"We're going kayaking."

He stared at Mia's kayak. I couldn't tell if he was excited or scared.

"I'll be right back."

He raced off to the cottage taking the iPad with him.

"Have you ever kayaked before?"

The boy shook his head.

"It's easier than riding a bike." I lifted the paddle and handed it to him. "Here."

He took the paddle.

I rotated the paddle in his hands. "You put your knuckles so that they're facing up just like the edges of the blades." I pushed his hands farther apart. I smiled and said, "Hands up."

He lifted his arms.

"You want your arms to be in right angles. You're making a square with your arms and the paddle." I adjusted his hands and then pulled his arms down in front of him. "That's good. The secret is to use your upper body to paddle. You want your arms to stay in the square."

I moved back. I pretended I held an imaginary paddle. I rotated my upper body. He mimicked my motions.

"You got it. Take your kayak down to the water."

One hand dragged the kayak while the other hand held the paddle. He stopped next to my kayak at the edge of the lake.

"Push it out some more."

He stood behind the kayak and pushed it farther into the water.

"OK, now straddle the boat."

He gave me his confused look.

"Hold the paddle. Put one foot on each side of the kayak and walk out. When you get above the cockpit, I want you to squat down."

He waddled with his feet astride the boat. The water went above his bare ankles.

"Sit down and put your feet inside."

He sat and pulled one knee up into the cockpit and then the other. He squirmed around until he felt comfortable. He turned to me. A smile and a look of "I'm really going to do this" filled his face.

I couldn't help smiling. "Dig the end of the paddle into the sand and push." I helped him free the kayak from the beach. "Make your square."

The boy positioned his hands like I taught him.

"Now, off you go."

He rotated and dipped the paddle into the water and off he went.

CHAPTER 24

I stood on the beach and watched as the boy got used to Mia's kayak. He was just like a kid with a new toy. I had forgotten what it was like to be his age. A time when everything was new and adventures were waiting to be discovered.

He paddled back and forth in front of our cottage. It took him awhile to be able to go in a straight line. He discovered a way to use the paddle to spin in a circle. With each new tiny conquest, there was a small look of triumph on his face.

I pushed my kayak into shallow water. I still love to kayak, but it is getting harder and harder to get in and out of the boat. When I was younger, I'd hop right in without thinking. Now, it was a major production.

I used the paddle like a walking stick for balance. I lifted one foot over the cockpit and straddled the kayak. The pain made me grimace as I sat. My knees were fine for swimming, but the arthritis had stolen my flexibility. I rested the paddle on the boat and then struggled to bend my knee far enough to get it into the cockpit. My left knee was worse than my right so I always did it first.

With both knees inside, I stretched my legs and waited for the pain to pass.

Mia was always after me to get a sit-on to replace my sit-in kayak. The sit-on had no cockpit so it would be much easier to get in and out of. But it was all open to the elements. The sit-on kayak gave you no shelter. Even small waves would soak you, which might be fine in August, but not in the frigid water of early spring.

I used the paddle to push off from the beach and went to join the boy.

We glided along the surface. There was no wind and the water was calm. We hugged the shore to stay away from the pontoon boats, which kept to the center of the lake. The pontoons were on their afternoon cruises. They traveled from our lake to the connecting lakes.

There were a few small skiffs with fishermen in the shallow water, but most of the true fishermen only fished in the early morning or at dusk. I fell into my natural rhythm. The boy had no trouble keeping up with me.

We came to the train trestle. This was the place where I would stop on my morning swim and then turn back for the cottage. I brought my paddle in and let the kayak glide. I sat back and stared up at the wooden slats above me. The tracks haven't been used for decades. The metal bridge was covered with rust. The boy's kayak came by my side.

I pointed up at the bridge that towered above us.

"When I was a kid it was a rite of passage. I was just about your age when I first jumped."

"No way," said Colin.

I swung my hand to an empty spot at the base of the trestle.

"Behind the landing there's a path that winds its way up to the train tracks. We'd come here in the evening as the sun was setting. We would jump one by one. You had to walk out to the center of the bridge before you jumped. That's the only spot where the water is deep enough. More than one boy got hurt because he didn't walk out far enough. Especially now in August you had to be careful. The lake's water level is low. Even in the center, when you jumped you had to bend your knees or there's a good chance you'd break your leg. That's what happened to Adam."

The boy gave me an incredulous look. "Why would you do it?"

It was a question that I always asked myself.

"I think we felt the need to prove to each other how brave we were."

The boy looked up at the bridge and shook his head. "Weren't you scared?"

"The first time I froze. I was petrified. I only jumped because Harry started laughing. I couldn't bear the shame."

"That's crazy."

"We were young, Colin. Teenagers do crazy things."

Chapter 25

For being a teacher, I'm really not much of a people person. Mia kept saying that she had to bring me out of my shell. Our social lives revolved around her friends and interests. She'd drag me along, but I was always much happier escaping into a good book, or like now, paddling my kayak.

The water quickened. I felt the pull of the stream. I nosed my kayak into the tributary that flowed off the lake. It was a shallow stream. For me it was always like entering a church. Tree branches arched and met above us. Sunlight danced through the leaves and undulated across the water. It was humid – almost like a sauna. You could smell the fecund soil lining the banks.

Like a church it was quiet and solemn. I let the flowing water take us. I only used the paddle to keep to the center of the stream. The boy was behind me. His face was flushed and bathed in sweat. He took his cap off and wiped his arm across his forehead. He nodded and I took that as a sign to go on.

We neared the bend in the stream. I wondered if they would be there.

Some churches have statues. My church has butterflies. We rounded the bend and there they were.

Milkweed plants grew wild along the bank. Hundreds of butterflies filled the air and hovered on the bushes. They were majestic and beautiful. Afternoon sunlight sparkled on vibrant wings as the butterflies fluttered from one spot to another. I don't know why they touched me so. I could sit here for hours and never tire of watching them.

I dug the edge of my paddle into the sand and used it like an anchor. I scooped water from the stream and bathed my face and neck. The boy stopped next to me and anchored. He refreshed his face and arms with water. It was as if he knew this was not a place to talk. He sat back in Mia's kayak. I watched his eyes as he watched the butterflies.

CHAPTER 26

We left my sanctuary. We left the humid air and intertwined overhead tree branches behind and came out into bright sunshine. The boy seemed more relaxed even though his skin was coated with sweat. As he paddled, he seemed to have found his natural rhythm. The sun was intense. With the heat, there was one more stop I wanted to make before we headed back to the cottage.

Our lake was a shallow lake, especially in August. Motorboats and pontoons had to be careful. More than one inexperienced captain had run aground on the sandbars lurking beneath the surface. The boat repair shop did a brisk business in replacing damaged propellers.

Those who had a boat and wanted to escape the intense heat of our late summer afternoons went to the Pointe. The sandbar was an extension of the forest that jutted out like a wedge into the lake. Just like a point, the slightly submerged sandbar went out 100 yards. Captains would drive the front of their pontoon boats right up onto the sand. The propellers would stay safe in the deeper water until it was time to push the pontoons back into the lake. At the end of the sandbar there was a passage wide and deep enough for two boats to slowly pass from one lake to the next. The passageway was marked with buoys and the bathers protected by a no-wake zone.

There was a line of pontoon boats docked on both sides of the sandbar. From a distance, it looked like boaters were walking on water. As if the lake was their own bathtub, toddlers sat on the sandbar submerged up to their tiny chests. I expected it to be crowded with the heat and I was right. It would be hard to find enough open space for another pontoon boat to dock on the sandbar, but it was easy to squeeze in two kayaks.

I paddled my kayak up onto the sand. Now came the hard part. I took my paddle and laid it behind me on the kayak's hull. I reached behind and gripped the paddle with each hand at my side. The secret was to use both hands in unison so that I wouldn't tip over. I used the paddle for leverage. I pushed down on the paddle and slid up and back to free my knees from the cockpit. I straddled the boat and used the paddle like a cane to stand.

I waved my hand and motioned the boy forward. He ran his kayak aground. I went to help him disembark, but he sprang out of the boat with agility that only the young possess. He didn't join me, but turned and ran into the lake. When he was deep enough, he dived and then surfaced. His hair flung beads of water as he shook his head. The water cooled him as I knew it would. He flashed me a look of happy contentment. He fell back and floated in the water.

I quickly remembered why I stopped coming to the sandbar. Everything was loud; too loud. Music blasted from speakers on the pontoon boat next to me. I didn't know the song, but then I don't listen to music. Teenagers shouted back and forth between the boats. There were shrieks of laughter. Middle-age couples sat on folding metal lawn chairs with their feet and calves submerged in the cool water. They talked animatedly while toasting each other with beers. Dogs pranced and barked on the deck of the boats for their masters to return.

It was too much. I had to get away. I took off my cap and slid off my white rash guard. I tossed them on top of the kayak. I walked into the lake and dived under the water. I held my breath as long as I could. Silence surrounded me.

I broke the surface and the boy was right there. He had his stricken look of concern that eased when I smiled at him.

"Where's your hat?"

He touched his head in disbelief. We both scanned the water.

I pointed. "There it is."

He swam and brought the cap back. The water was shallow enough that we could both stand. He stood and put the Mud Hens cap back on. The buzz came from behind him. Three Jet Skis were zigzagging across the lake. They were like kids playing a game of tag, but these were lethal machines. They were watching each other, not the water.

I shook my head in disgust and walked back to the sandbar. The music and shouting and buzz of Jet Skis were too much for me. I tossed my shirt and cap in the kayak. I pulled the boat into the water. I almost fell as I tried to get in, but the boy's hands saved me. I didn't even know he was by me.

The kayak rocked. I used my paddle for balance. I ignored the pain in my knees. I got into the boat. I didn't wait for the boy. I had to get away.

Chapter 27

I awoke disorientated. I was in my chair on the porch. My finger was still inside the book that I was reading, marking my progress. It was Hemingway's *A Moveable Feast*. I never tired of reading him. No matter how many times I read one of his books, I always learned something new. I liked to compare my Paris to the Paris he wrote about in *A Moveable Feast*, but then he had no comparison for my Mia.

I don't wear a watch and there wasn't a clock on the porch. I used the angle of the outside sunlight to try and judge the time. It had to be close to dinnertime. The boy must be starving.

The cottage was quiet. I set the book aside and pushed up from the chair. My knees ached in protest. I tried to ignore the pain. I went and knocked on the boy's door.

"Colin."

I opened the door. He was sprawled on top of his bed. His eyes darted from his game to me and then back to his game.

"Hungry?"

I had his interest. The game paused and he stared at me.

"There's not much here. I could order a pizza. There's a place that delivers."

His eyes lit up. "That'd be great."

"What do you like on it?"

"Anything but anchovies."

"Medium or large?"

"Do they have extra large?"

I laughed, but then I realized he wasn't kidding.

"I'll see."

"And pop." He gave me a look of longing filled with hope. "Can they deliver Mountain Dew?"

I laughed again.

"I'll see."

He devoured four sizes of pizza and washed it down with Mountain Dew. Mia would not be happy with our food choice. She was a health addict long before it became fashionable. Fruits and vegetables were our mainstay. Our only meats were chicken or turkey. We ate plenty of fish, even though neither of us were fishermen.

The health addict in me wasn't diet it was always exercise. Since I was a teenager, I worked out every day. In my youth it was weights and running. Now it was mainly swimming with an occasional kayak trip. When the weather would turn against me, I'd drive the 10 miles to the YMCA in the city and use the indoor pool.

The boy eyed the two pieces left in the box.

"You're going to explode." I closed the box and pulled it closer to me.

He shrugged and reached for his ever present iPad. I needed to catch him before he vanished into his fantasy world.

"I was so much like you at your age."

He pulled his iPad closer and impatiently tapped his fingers on it.

"One day I got out of the shower and looked in the mirror. I didn't like the boy who stared back at me. That boy wasn't who I wanted to be. I wanted to be strong. I wanted to like the person who stared back at me. It took me a long time to realize that the only person who could change that boy was me."

He stared at his iPad as his fingers drummed.

I don't think he understood what I was trying to tell him. Maybe he was too young or maybe I was just turning into a foolish old man.

I took the pizza box and put it in the refrigerator. I turned back to the table. The boy was gone.

CHAPTER 28

It would be another scorcher. I finished my swim and climbed the ladder. The wooden deck was already hot to the touch beneath my bare feet. The sky was cloudless. The sun was hot and bright. It quickly sucked moisture from my skin as I walked to the cottage.

We seemed to have fallen into a routine. The boy sat at the kitchen table. He glanced at me and poured another bowl of cereal. His ever-present iPad was off to the side.

I went and poured a glass of orange juice from the fridge. I grabbed my morning banana and sat across from him.

He asked between mouthfuls, "What are we going to do today?"

"I don't know. Are you sore?"

He gave me his questioning stare.

"Your shoulders. All that kayaking. Do you hurt?"

He rolled his shoulders. "A little."

"That's good. You're building muscles. Couple more weeks and you'll be the envy of every boy at school."

He laughed. It was good to hear him laugh. I'd be happy for just a smile.

I peeled my banana. "I already got my exercise. Why don't you take the kayak out?"

His spoon froze above the cereal bowl.

"By myself?"

"You told me you're 13. You know how to swim. Just stay close to shore and stay on the lake. Don't go off on any of the streams. You'll be fine."

He swallowed. I saw the struggle reflected in his face. I knew I was asking him to step out of his safe place.

I put bravado in my voice. "It'll be an adventure."

I made sure he had a water bottle. The boy put sunblock on his arms, face and neck. He wore his swimsuit, T-shirt, and his cap. He had a look of determination as he climbed into the kayak.

"The water's calm. Keep an eye on the sky. It's clear now and it'll probably stay that way all day. If it gets cloudy, come back home. It doesn't take long for a storm to form. When you get away from the cottage get your bearings." I pointed to the house next door. "The Petersons' cottage has a copper roof. The sun reflects off it. When you're out on the lake you can't miss it. It's like a lighthouse that'll bring you home."

The boy took a sip of water and set the bottle between his legs.

"Don't be gone too long. Just remember, however far you paddle, that's how far you're going to have to paddle to get back."

He lifted the paddle. "I'll be fine. I'm going on an adventure."

He was a smart one. He used my own words. We both smiled. I pushed him off. The kayak rocked until he got settled.

I wanted to stay on the dock and watch him for as long as I could. But I didn't want him to feel that I was like his mother hovering over him.

I turned away from the boy and walked from the dock. I sat on my Adirondack chair. The boy had already paddled down the coast and was out of view.

I glanced to the water where Mia rested. She would not have approved. She would have wanted me go with him. We would have argued. I would have told her the boy needed to grow. He needed to become himself. She would have told me that he's just a boy.

Maybe we were both right. I fought the urge to get in my kayak and chase after him.

Chapter 29

I figured he'd be gone for a few minutes or a few hours. He would either like being out on the lake by himself or he wouldn't. After 15 minutes I got up from my chair and went into the cottage. There were bills that needed to be paid.

An hour passed and then two. With each minute, I grew more anxious. I walked down to the dock. I cupped my hands above my eyes to block the sun. I saw plenty of boats on the lake, but I didn't see Mia's kayak.

I could get into my kayak and try to follow him. If he decided to circle the lake it would be a fool's errand. I'd chase after him only to have him beat me home.

The sense of helplessness was too much. I felt like I was back in the room with Mia where there was nothing I could do but wait.

I went and sat on my chair and waited.

He came from the right into my field of vision. He had a smooth stroke. He used his upper body like I taught him. He steered the kayak to the shore. He climbed out and dragged the boat up on the beach. Our eyes met. He waited to see how I would react.

The sense of relief that he was back and safe overwhelmed me. I knew I had to be smiling because he returned the smile.

He lifted the water bottle from the kayak and took a deep swallow. He wiped his wrist across his mouth. I glimpsed the man he could become.

"You were right. I could see the roof shining from across the lake. It is like a beacon."

"You were gone a long time."

"Were you worried?"

His question trapped me so I didn't answer.

"Mom always makes me take my cell phone. When I'm away from home, she calls me every 10 minutes."

"I'm not your mom."

He smiled. "I know."

He slid the paddle into the kayak and pulled the boat behind him. He winced as his bare foot stepped on a pebble.

"We need to get you some surf shoes."

"Surf shoes?"

"They're like moccasins. You can get them wet. They'll protect the bottom of your feet."

"Does Churchill's sell them?"

"Churchill's sells everything. Come on, let's get you some lunch. You must be starving."

He left the kayak and walked up the path to join me. I don't know why, I felt the urge to put my arm around his shoulder, but I did. He seemed surprised by the gesture, but he didn't pull away from me.

We walked to the cottage together.

CHAPTER 30

Colin changed out of his sweat-stained T-shirt and damp swimsuit while I searched the cupboards for food. We were in luck. We had some pancake mix and some eggs in the fridge.

The boy sat at the kitchen table and inhaled pancakes as fast as I could make them.

"So how was it, your great adventure?"

"It's so different from LA. The air's so fresh. It's like I can breathe. You don't have smog like we do. Some days it gets so bad, they tell people to stay inside." He smothered his pancakes with butter. "I stopped at the Pointe. It wasn't as crowded as yesterday."

"It's only really bad on the weekends."

"I pulled the kayak ashore and swam for a while to cool off. We have the ocean in LA, but I'm scared to go in it. The beach might be good for surfing, but it's not good for swimming. The waves are too rough and even in the summer the water's cold. And then there's always the danger of being caught by a rip current and pulled out to sea."

"In LA?"

He nodded emphatically and swallowed.

"And then you have to worry about sharks."

"Sharks?" I laughed.

"It's true. There's always someone on the news getting eaten by sharks."

I asked again, "In LA?"

He poured syrup on the pancakes. "Well, in the ocean." He forked two pieces of pancakes and pointed them at me. "Why don't you fish?"

I had forgotten how teenagers jump from one thought to another with no rhyme or reason.

"I've never had the patience." I looked up from the pancakes I was cooking. "Do you want to fish?"

He shrugged his shoulders. "If you fished, you could catch and eat your own dinner."

"That's what many people do here."

"That's pretty cool."

"It is if you have the patience."

He gave me his quizzical look as he pondered my last sentence.

"You like to play with words."

"I taught English and literature."

I felt like we were each trying to find out who the other person was. I slid more pancakes onto his plate.

"That's the last of them."

"Don't you want any?"

"I already ate."

"They're good."

"Anything's good when you're hungry."

"Are you going to stay here?"

Another question out of the blue, but this one was easy to answer.

"Where else would I go? This is my home."

CHAPTER 31

I had forgone my morning swim. I would only have the boy for so many days and there were so many things I wanted to show him.

I sat in my chair reading on the porch. He did a double take when he saw me from the kitchen.

He ambled over and leaned against the doorway. He held his iPad loosely in his hand. I wondered if he slept in his clothes. I realized doing a load of laundry was another chore to add to my list.

"Are you sick?"

I was surprised by the concern in his voice.

"No, I'm fine."

"Why didn't you swim?"

"I wanted to save my energy for later."

He didn't give in to the obvious question, but waited with an expectant look.

"I thought we would go on a hike, another adventure."

He mulled the offer.

"How long would we be gone?"

"All day."

He practically screeched, "All day?"

"It's a long hike to where we're going."

He glanced down at his iPad.

"Today will be a real adventure."

He looked at me and sharply said, "There you go with your words again."

I couldn't help but laugh.

"Get yourself something to eat. You'll need the energy."

He stood for a moment or two weighing his choices. He gave me his boyish shrug, which I took for acquiescence. He turned and walked to the kitchen.

The boy didn't bring any long pants. He said in summer all the kids in California just wears shorts. I gave him a pair of Mia's hiking socks. The socks covered his calves. His cargo shorts came down to his knees. He looked like a Swiss boy ready to go hiking in the Alps. I figured he'd be fine. He didn't have boots so his gym shoes would have to do.

I went to the closet and took out our walking staffs. They were strong and sturdy. A craftsman in town carved them. He searched the forests that surrounded our lakes for the perfect pieces of wood. Mine was made from oak and Mia's from hickory. They were things of beauty. The craftsman had drilled a hole in the top of the staffs so that we both had a strap to wrap around our wrist. I took my staff and put Mia's back.

The boy quipped, "Are you going to turn into a wizard?"

"Before the day's out, I'm going to be glad that I have it."

I put a couple of water bottles and protein power bars into the backpack. I took the first aid kit from the cupboard and slid it inside. I handed the backpack to Colin. I grabbed the bug spray. I pushed the boy toward the door.

In the yard, I sprayed the boy and then gave him the bottle to spray me. Colin hoisted the backpack onto his shoulders. I slid the bug spray into one of the pouches.

I stepped back and took stock. If Mia were here, she would take a picture of the boy. There was a beguiling smile beneath the Mud Hens cap and a hint of excitement in his eyes.

"We're off."

Chapter 32

The forest always made me feel like a child. We walked in shadows as trees towered above us and swaying leaves blocked the sunlight. I led and the boy followed. We walked paths worn down by centuries of deer hooves, moccasins, and gym shoes.

I stopped and leaned on my staff. There was so much to see and hear. Saplings struggled to grow in the shade of enormous oaks that were much older than me. Bushy tailed squirrels scampered on branches that creaked with the wind. Crows cawed. And then there were the colors. Forget waterlilies, Monet should have painted in a forest. There were hundreds of different shades of green on the leaves and brown on the barks.

I tilted my head and gazed to the sky. Chicago had its skyscrapers, I had my trees.

The boy was patient. He didn't fidget, but stood quietly beside me. I wondered if he could lose himself the way I did in the beauty and solitude of the forest. We continued our journey.

"Aren't you worried about forest fires?"

I almost laughed, but his voice was serious. I

remembered where he came from. I stopped and turned toward him.

"Feel the air."

"What?"

"Breathe in." I demonstrated. I inhaled through my nose. My chest expanded. I exhaled. "The air is cool and moist."

He inhaled and held it as if he tried to taste the air.

"It's not like California. We're surrounded by lakes big and small. We get over 30 inches of precipitation a year. It averages out that it rains or snows one out of every three days. We don't have droughts the way you do in California. Don't worry about forest fires."

He seemed satisfied. We continued on. The ground steepened. I made use of my walking staff. We walked at a leisurely pace stopping every so often to ponder. The minutes turned to hours. My left knee ached. I hoped there was ibuprofen in the first aid kit.

We stopped at the top of a small rise. I waited and listened. It didn't take long. The noise was so out of place in the forest.

The boy turned in a circle. "Where is it?"

I didn't answer. I kept walking. We rounded the bend. The path suddenly ended at a two-lane paved road. A truck streaked by going 50 miles per hour. The trailing wind blew the boy's cap off. He quickly looked down the road and then hustled to get it. I followed and took Colin's arm. I pulled him across the asphalt to the dilapidated wooden structure.

The diner was like Churchill's: a fixture that went

back to my childhood. It looked like a large log cabin. It was set back from the road on a gravel parking lot. There were pickup trucks parked haphazardly in the lot. There was a wooden hand-painted sign that hung from a post out by the road. It was so small that passing trucks couldn't possibly read *Walt's Diner*. Like Churchill's, the business relied on local patrons to survive.

I walked up onto the wooden porch. There were two rocking chairs by the door facing the road. An old man sat in one chair reading his newspaper. His coffee mug rested on a small table by his side. He looked up above the reading glasses perched on the end of his nose and nodded. I and the boy nodded back. I shooed some flies away from the screen door. I opened the door and the boy and I walked inside.

Chapter 33

I watched the boy as he entered the room. His blue eyes widened as he saw the stags. There were a dozen male deer heads mounted on the walls each with an impressive rack of antlers. Their eyes were frozen and lifelike.

The boy drew a breath and said, "I guess vegetarians don't come here for lunch."

I laughed. I handed him my staff. "Take it and put it in the corner out of the way."

A few of the tables were occupied. I went and sat at one of the many remaining empty tables strewn around the room. Colin came and sat across from me.

"Did you think I was going to let you starve?"

"I thought we were going to be real hikers and survive on protein bars."

I wondered where this new boy and his sense of humor had been hiding.

Everything was dark wood in the diner: scratched floors, scarred tables, and rickety chairs. Light came from fluorescent fixtures that were hung from the ceiling joists and hummed above our heads.

Millie came from behind the counter. She was gray haired and slightly stooped and older than me. She sat on the chair beside me and took my hand.

"I'm so sorry, Emmet."

"I am too."

"When I lost Walt, I didn't think I could go on, but you do. You do Emmet. You do go on."

Not trusting myself to speak, I just nodded.

Millie glanced across the table and brightened "And who's this?"

"My grandson, Colin, from California. He's staying with me for a couple of weeks."

"He's got your eyes and Jackie's nose."

Colin seemed surprised to hear his mother's name.

The screen door slammed. Two men walked into the restaurant. All they were missing were their fishing rods.

Millie said, "I have to get back to work. You want your usual."

"I do."

"And the boy, should I bring him a big venison steak."

A look of horror appeared on the Colin's face.

Millie and I laughed.

"I think he's more of a cheeseburger, fries, and milkshake boy. Am I right, Colin?"

He shook his head vigorously. "That's me."

Millie set her hand on my shoulder and used me as leverage to stand. She squeezed my shoulder, then walked to the fishermen.

CHAPTER 34

Colin dipped a fry in ketchup. "What sort of name is Emmet? I don't know anyone with that name."

"It's Irish. I was named after my grandfather, who was named after his grandfather. Robert Emmet was an Irish patriot. He was part of Ireland's continuous rebellion against British tyranny. He was captured, hung, and beheaded by the British in 1803. He was supposed to have said as he stood on the gallows, 'Let no man write my epitaph. When my country takes her place among the nations of the earth, then and not till then, let my epitaph be written.' In Ireland boys are named after him to preserve his memory."

I snatched one of Colin's last French fries and held it in front of me. "Our ancestors fled Ireland during the potato famine way back in the 1840s. My grandfather's grandfather, our first Emmet, survived the journey. His parents never set foot in America. They died, like so many others, on one of the famine ships. So many died on the the ships carrying the Irish to America that they came to be known as coffin ships. They say sharks used to follow the ships across the ocean as they tossed off the dead. Emmet was just a boy about your age. He and his brothers were stranded in New York."

I looked at my grandson. "You think it's hard being a teenager today? Emmet and his brothers were stranded in a strange land. They had no money, no friends, no skills, and no education."

I slowly ate the French fry.

"So what happened to them?"

"The boys spent the next 10 years working their way across the country as common laborers. They dug ditches for the canals and worked on the railroad. They finally saved enough money to buy a small farm in Iowa. They worked hard and when the harvests were good they bought more land."

I pushed back from the table and stretched my legs. "The second Emmet, my grandfather, was the first Hyland to graduate from high school. I was the first Hyland to graduate from college." I studied my grandson. "And hopefully not the last."

The boy's mood changed. His mouth tightened and his eyes hardened.

"It's important to know your ancestry. To know whose blood flows in you."

The boy snapped, "I'm not a Hyland. My name is Colin Becker."

I don't know where the anger came from. "You have my blood in you. That makes you a Hyland to me."

His face reddened. His suppressed rage was almost tangible. If we were home, I knew he would stomp off to his room and his game.

"I'm going to pay the bill. Why don't you get my stick and meet me outside."

I didn't wait for his answer. I left him alone and walked over to Millie.

CHAPTER 35

I let the boy walk ahead of me. We continued our journey. We went deep into the woods. The walk seemed to drain the anger out of the boy. It's hard to stay angry when you're surrounded by beauty.

At the top of a small rise, the boy stopped and gazed around. Thick, towering trees surrounded him and blocked out the sunlight.

He waited for me to catch up to him and then asked, "Aren't you afraid of getting lost?"

"You won't get lost as long as you stay on the path."

He gave me his challenging look. "What happens when the paths cross? How do you know which one to take?"

"You don't. That's why you don't come out here by yourself. You need a guide – someone who has been here before to show you the way."

He came back quickly. "And who was your guide?" He studied my face and waited.

I wouldn't lie to the boy.

"My father."

He nodded. He had the answer he wanted. He didn't say anything. He stared off into the distance. I don't know if it was hurt or anger that made him worry his lower lip like his mother would when she was troubled.

I thought of all the things I could say, but I felt my words would just be banalities. I couldn't bring his father back. I wouldn't even try.

"It's not much farther."

I walked around him and continued down the path.

My knee ached. I was afraid this would happen. I could feel it swell. I used my staff to try and take the weight off my left leg. The boy had gotten ahead of me. He seemed lost in his own thoughts. If he rounded the bend, I would lose sight of him.

"Colin."

He didn't hear me so I shouted, "Colin!"

Crows cawed and scattered from the branches. The boy jogged back to me.

He huffed out, "Are you OK?"

"I'm fine. I just need a drink of water."

He came closer and slid off the backpack.

"I need the first aid kit too."

He studied me suspiciously. He took the kit from the pack and held it out. I opened the kit and found a packet of ibuprofen inside. He watched me as I opened the packet and swallowed two pills. He took a water bottle from the pack, twisted off the cap and handed it to me.

"You're OK?"

"My knee hurts. It happens all the time. It's no big deal."

"Should we go home?"

"We came all this way." I pointed ahead. "What I want to show you is just around the bend. We'll finish what we started." I planted my staff and pushed off.

The boy swung the pack back up on his shoulders. He hovered at my side as we walked forward.

CHAPTER 36

At the bend, the main path continued and a smaller, less-traveled path veered off to the side.

"Watch for poison ivy."

"What does it look like?"

I didn't answer, but led the boy down the smaller path. It wasn't long before I found what I was looking for. I used the tip of my staff to gently touch the bush.

"See how the three green leaves grew close together out of the same stem. That's poison ivy. Beware of any three-leaved bush."

The boy took a step back.

"Like I said before, just stay on the path and you'll be fine."

We walked a little farther and then I stopped. I looked at the boy and waited.

He opened his mouth but then swallowed the question. He gazed around and then closed his eyes.

"Water. A brook? A stream?"

I smiled. "Let's find out."

The soothing rhythmic cadence of flowing water grew louder as we walked the path.

It wasn't a proper waterfall like the ones they have in Northern Michigan, but it was ours. Water rippled over rocks and fell a few feet into a deep pond. There was an outcropping of large rocks off to the side that captured the afternoon sun. It was our own private Shangri-La.

"Strip down to your skivvies and jump in."

The boy laughed. "Skivvies?"

"You kids still wear underwear don't you?"

From his face, I knew the boy wondered if I was testing him. I nodded. He slid the backpack from his shoulders. He sat and pulled off his gym shoes and Mia's socks. He stood and turned away from me and peeled off his shirt and slid down his shorts. I guessed the days of tighty whities had passed. He wore blue checkered boxers.

"It's deep. Just take a running start and jump right in."

He didn't hesitate. He ran forward a few steps and jumped. He hit the water with a large splash and quickly sank beneath the surface. He sprang up just as quickly.

He shouted, "It's friggin cold."

"You'll get used to it."

I relied on my staff on the uneven ground as I walked around the pond to the rocks. There was a long, flat rock right at the edge of the water. It was in full sunlight only inches above the earth around it. I stepped up on the ledge. I wanted to shed my clothes and join the boy, but it would be too much of a struggle to get out of my hiking boots and jeans. Even if I got my boots off, I don't know if I could bend my left knee far enough to get them back on. I would have to ask the boy for help. I didn't want to do that.

I used the staff to ease down on top of the rock. I settled and stretched my legs out in front of me. My knee throbbed. I felt the swelling. Even under my jeans the knee felt hot. I'd pack it in ice when we got home. I wasn't looking forward to the long walk back.

The boy was exploring. He dived and tried to reach the bottom. He swam and disappeared under the overhanging ledges. He reappeared and then treaded water under the cascading fall.

He seemed happy. That made the whole trip worthwhile. It was another memory that I would add to the many of this magical place in the woods.

CHAPTER 37

My mind wandered and the memories returned as poignant as ever. I could see Mia standing in front of me. She would tease me with her smile and then waste no time. She'd quickly step out of her clothes and dive into the water.

I was the bashful one who always worried that someone would stumble upon us. Mia would swim naked with abandon in the pond. She was my siren who lured me to the deep. There was no way I could resist her. No way that I wanted to.

The boy stood in front of me dripping water. His concerned look was back on his face. He held the backpack in one hand and his clothes in the other.

I tapped the rock. "Lie down. The sun will dry you in no time."

He sat next to me. He leaned back and used the backpack as a pillow.

"How'd you find this place?"

"Your grandma led me here. When I had asked her how she found it, she gave me her mysterious smile, but never answered."

"Didn't you bug her about it?"

"I thought about it, but then I thought sometimes it's best not to know the answer."

"You miss her?"

Another question out of the blue. How do I put in words how I feel?

"You have to understand, Colin. Mia was my friend before we became lovers. Becoming lovers only added to our friendship. We were friends for 50 years. I miss her every moment. I don't know how to live my life without her."

I turned away from the boy. I chastised myself: you silly old man you can't cry in front of your grandson. I drew a breath. My finger wiped the tears from my cheeks.

I turned back to the boy. "We're not meant to live alone. You have to find your friend, Colin. That's what makes you whole."

CHAPTER 38

The boy lay in the sun. His body glistened with water droplets. I knew he thought about my words. The sun was bright on his face. He covered his eyes with his arm. I watched the rise and fall of his young chest. Part of me was jealous. I envied his youth. With age comes wisdom, but also decrepitness. How I wished I could recapture the vitality of youth. His face relaxed. I wondered if he drifted off to sleep. I'd let him rest for a while. It was a long walk back to the cottage.

It should have been an easier walk coming home from the waterfall. The falls were higher than the lake. Going to the falls we struggled uphill. The way back was a gentle downhill slope. But my left knee throbbed. With each step it felt like the bones were grinding together. I used my walking staff like a crutch. I walked slower and slower. The boy would glance at me, but he wouldn't say anything.

I felt the change in the air. The canopy of leaves was thick overhead and blocked out the sky. No sunbeams tried to peek through. I knew the clouds must have rolled in. Even in the forest, I could smell rain in the air. It wasn't long until there was the pitter-patter of raindrops on the leaves above us.

The boy titled his head up and gazed in curiosity at the swaying leaves. A few raindrops made it through the canopy and fell beside us.

"It's a good thing you've got your hat. This is going to be a soaker."

"How do you know?"

"Do you feel the wind?"

The boy stood still.

"A little."

"Do you hear thunder?"

The boy tilted and then shook his head.

"There's no reason to be scared. It's a slow moving storm. We don't have to worry about lightning, but we'll be drenched before we get home."

"Why would I be scared? I'm with you aren't I?"

I laughed and the boy smiled.

Colin slid the backpack from his shoulder and took out a protein bar. He opened it and handed the bar to me.

I took it and nodded my thanks. He took a bar for himself and slid the backpack back onto his shoulders.

We were wet, but not soaked when we came to the road. We'd have to leave the shelter of the trees. Walt's Diner was beckoning as a safe harbor from the rain, but a stop there would just put off the inevitable. The rain wasn't going to stop and darkness was coming.

We walked out into the downpour and stopped at the side of the road. A car whizzed by. The trailing sheet of water soaked us even more. Rain rolled off the rim of the boy's cap. Throughout the entire walk, I hadn't heard one word of complaint. Maybe it was an adventure for him. We crossed the road. There was some shelter from the downpour as we re-entered the woods.

"You know the way home from here. Why don't you run ahead?"

"No."

I waited for him to elaborate, but he wouldn't. I pushed him.

"Go."

He snapped back, "I'm not leaving you."

I saw my grandson in a different light. The boy had grit.

"OK."

The hardest part of the walk was when we left the woods. The exposed path along the lake was soaked and in some parts it was a muddy quagmire.

The boy suddenly stopped and looked back. His tennis shoe was stuck in the mud. He tried to hop on one foot back to the shoe. He lost his balance and down he went. He quickly rolled over onto his hands and knees.

I couldn't help it, I laughed. Covered in mud, he was a slight. The boy sat back and pulled off his other shoe and then grabbed both shoes and stood.

I couldn't stop laughing.

"It's not funny."

I huffed between laughs, "Oh, but it is."

He tried to shake the mud from his hands and shoes. He gave up and wiggled his toes in the mud. He looked at me. His face changed and suddenly he laughed.

We stood in the downpour and laughed.

CHAPTER 39

I had the boy strip off his muddy clothes in the laundry room and then sent him to the shower. I knew he wouldn't come out until the hot water was all gone. I'd have to wait until morning to take my shower. I changed into a dry T-shirt and shorts and limped into the kitchen. I filled a clear plastic bag with ice and then used an Ace bandage to wrap it around my knee. I took three ibuprofens and washed them down with a glass of water.

I went out to the porch and sat on my chair. I propped my leg up on a stool. Rain drummed on the roof. I tried to read, but my eyes grew heavy.

I awoke disorientated in the dark. It took me awhile to recognize the sound. It seemed so out of place in a cottage by the lake. It slowly dawned on me it had to be the boy's game.

The ice had melted. I unwound the bag from my knee. The swelling was down, but now the knee was stiff. I hobbled to the kitchen.

"Why didn't you wake me? You must be starving."

The boy paused his game and looked up from his seat

at the kitchen table. He glanced guiltily to two empty boxes of macaroni and cheese on the counter.

"Oh."

The boy asked with concern, "How's your knee?"

I pulled a chair out and sat down. "It's better."

His hand hovered over his iPad.

I shook my head. "I don't understand the fascination that you have with your game."

The boy lifted the iPad so that I could see the screen. "It's not hard to understand. When I play the game, I don't have to think about anything else. I just play the game."

"Is it that you don't have to think?" I searched his face as I asked, "Or that you don't have to feel?"

"What difference does it make? Think? Feel? I'm not here. I go into a different world."

"You can't run away from life."

He asked mockingly, "You can't? You do it all the time." He pointed his finger at my chair. "You sit on the porch and read your books."

"Reading is different."

He snapped, "You don't escape into another world when you read?"

"I do, but when I come back, I know how to live in this world."

His eyes stopped me. I felt like he wanted to lash out. His knuckles whitened as he gripped his game.

I tried to calm him. I said softly, "Colin, everyone has their escape mechanism. There's nothing the matter with that as long as you realize it's just a respite, a chance to escape for a while from the stress in your life."

He shouted, "You make it sound so easy." He jabbed his fingers to the lake. "You have your perfect life here. You have no idea what my life is like."

He took his game and fled.

I shouted, "Colin."

The bedroom door slammed. If the boy was like his mother, I would hear him hitting and kicking the walls. The cottage was silent.

I waited. It wasn't long before I heard the squeak of the mattress as he sat on the bed and then the beeps from his game.

CHAPTER 40

The rain had stopped. The air was saturated with moisture. Fog like ethereal clouds hovered over the lake. I had to swim.

I had swum the same lap for so long that I could navigate my way in the morning twilight. I knew the lake's many moods. Today she was full and sassy. There was a slight chop on the water. I knew her different currents just like I knew the different parts of my body. I swam. The water embraced me and took the stiffness from my joints. I breathed in rhythm with the waves.

I finished my swim. The sun was out and the sky was bright. The sparkling lake was empty and quiet, but I knew it wouldn't last. It was only a matter of time until the Jet Skis awakened.

I didn't swim to the dock, but to Mia. I treaded water until I got my bearings. I hyperventilated and then dived. It took a long time to find her and when I did I couldn't stay. She was disappearing, returning to the water and the sand. I knew it wouldn't be long until I would find no trace of her.

My chest ached. I broke to the surface. I treaded water. The boy sat on the dock.

I swam to him and held onto the ladder.

He leaned over and asked, "Can I take the kayak out?"

The boy was like his mother. She would throw a fit and get it out of her system and then come back as if nothing had happened. He was dressed in his swimsuit and T-shirt. His Mud Hens cap shaded his eyes.

I climbed the ladder. My knee ached in protest.

"Where do you want to go?"

The boy stood and said, "I don't know. I just want to go kayaking."

I searched the sky. It was bright blue and cloudless with only a slight breeze.

"You have sunblock on?"

"I'll put some on."

He looked at me expectantly. I wondered how many times his mother denied his requests.

"Have fun. Be safe."

He smiled in triumph. He ran to the cottage to put on the sunblock.

I walked along the dock. I sat in my Adirondack chair. The lake was coming alive. Pontoon boats glided to the Pointe. Power boats roared and Jet Skis buzzed. Angry waves lapped against my feet.

The boy ran past me without a glance. A water bottle was clutched in his hand. He pushed Mia's kayak into the lake. He grabbed the paddle and jumped in. He scooted down into the cabin. He pushed away from shore. He spun the kayak in a circle and faced me. He waved.

I held my hand up and then made a shooing motion. I don't know why, but he waited a moment. If Mia were here, she'd take a picture. I didn't need a camera. I had my own album of memories.

The boy dug the edge of the paddle into the water. He slowly spun away from me. He easily found his rhythm. He had more strength than I thought. The kayak smoothly glided across the lake.

I watched until he disappeared around the bend. I sat back in my chair. The boy would only be here for a few more days. I suddenly realized how much I was going to miss him.

CHAPTER 41

I slammed my book down onto the end table. I couldn't read. The high-pitched whine brought me from the porch. There were three sleek, black Jet Skis zigzagging on the lake in front of the dock. They were like motorcycles on water. They shot water high into the air like the crests of roosters. The riders all wore life vests. They cut across each other's wake to see how high they could jump their crafts. One boat went almost vertical. The driver hung on as the boat crashed back to the water.

Not to be outdone, the second boater revved his Jet Ski. He brought the bow up out of the water and spun it in a circle. All I could think of was a rodeo cowboy riding a bucking bronc. He overspun and the Jet Ski flipped. The engine died. The rider must have been tossed, which yanked out the cord to the safety cutoff switch. I quickly went to the end of the dock. The Jet Ski blocked my view. I couldn't see the rider. I hoped he wasn't trapped under the boat.

The two other Jet Skis raced back. The boats slowed and circled. A black clad figure climbed out of the water onto the bottom of the overturned Jet Ski. He grabbed the bottom edge of the boat and slipped back, righting his personal watercraft. He held onto the boat and moved to the boat's stern. He climbed up.

There were shouts and laughter. The rider sat and re-engaged the cord to the kill switch that tethered him to the boat. The engine whined and the others joined in. They shattered the solitude of the lake. Like angry wasps, the Jet Skis sped away.

I noticed the boy. He was at the edge of my vision. He paddled just enough to keep his kayak in place. I wondered how long he had watched the scene play out. I wondered what he thought of the Jet Skis. Did he hate them like I did or did he want the thrill of riding one?

CHAPTER 42

My bladder woke me. I figured it must be 2 or 3 in the morning. The cottage was silent. I quietly went and peed. I came back to bed, but sleep eluded me. My mind kicked in and I knew it would be hours before sleep returned. It would do no good to stay in bed and toss and turn. I got out of bed and walked from the porch to the lake. I stood on the dock and looked to the sky. The stars were out. I would wake the boy.

I opened the bedroom door. The room was stuffy and filled with the boy's smell. He should sleep with the door open, but teenage boys liked their privacy. The boy was on his side sprawled on top of the blankets with a pillow clutched against his stomach. His iPad was beside the pillow. He wore the same clothes he wore during the day. His snores were like his voice – some deep tones some light.

I gently shook his shoulder. "Colin."

He was deep in sleep. I shook harder and said louder, "Colin."

He gulped a snore. He stirred and then turned away from me.

I put some steel in my voice. "Wake up." I shook him. "There's something I want you to see."

He rolled back to me. His eyes opened. It took a while to chase the dreams away and for him to focus.

"What's the matter?"

"There's something I want you to see. Meet me outside by the kayaks."

I backed away and waited in the doorway. The boy swung his legs over the side of the bed. He grabbed his pillow and put it in his lap. He rocked back and forth.

"What time is it?"

"Don't worry about the time." I waited. He continued rocking. "You're not going to go back to sleep?"

"I'm up." He waved me away. "Give me a few minutes."

I left him alone.

The stars were bright. I wouldn't need a flashlight. I walked from the cottage to the dock and waited. It wasn't long until the boy appeared. He had put on his Mud Hens cap. He walked tentatively down the porch steps. He had probably turned the light on in the bathroom. It would take a while to regain his night vision.

I walked from the dock to the kayaks. I pulled out my paddle. I pushed the boat into shallow water. I straddled the kayak and ignored the pain in my knee as I climbed into the cockpit. I pushed away from shore.

The boy was quicker and more fluid than me. It wasn't long until his kayak was next to mine.

There was no need to whisper, but I did anyway. "Just follow me."

I waited for his question, but he stayed silent. There was no wind and without any other boats on the lake, the water was like glass. I dipped my paddle into the stillness. Ripples floated back to shore.

I kept an easy pace. The boy stayed slightly back and to my right side. The kayaks glided silently across the water. I felt like a boy again sneaking out of the cottage to rendezvous with my friends.

CHAPTER 43

The lake doesn't change. In light or darkness everything remains in place. We followed the familiar contour of the shore. There were occasional security lights on the docks glowing like beacons. A few lights shined from within the lake houses either forgotten to be turned off or used by insomniacs. I left the shore and headed for deeper water. The boy followed and we left the lights behind.

We paddled across the lake with our strokes in union. Through the starlight, I could just make out the dark woods on the far shore. I knew we weren't far from where I wanted to go. I picked up speed. The kayak flew across the still water. My muscles burned, but it was a good hurt.

The boy stayed with me. I knew we were close. I prepared for the jolt and then it came. The kayak hit and slid up upon the sandbar. The momentum rocked me forward. I bounced back. The boy hit the sandbar next to me. I laughed at his startled face.

Colin looked around. He dug his paddle into the sand.

"The Pointe?" he asked.

"Many a boat had run aground here. You can't see the variations of the water in the dark."

"I knew it had to be here somewhere, but still I didn't see it."

"You can't in starlight. Let's go for a walk."

I put my paddle behind me on the kayak and pushed up and out of the boat. I stood on the sand. Water soaked my surf shoes. I pulled the kayak farther up on the sandbank. The boy did what I did, only quicker. I walked on the sand. Water lapped my ankles.

Our lake was far out in the country in rural Michigan. There was no glow of lights from a town or city on the horizon. The few lights from shore were like pinpricks of light peeping through a dark blanket. We walked along the sandbar out into the lake.

We were far from shore. Still, dark water surrounded us.

I stopped and said, "Look above you."

I had no need to see the stars. I needed to see the boy's face. Colin titled his head back. His face filled with wonder. His smile was a sight to behold. I wondered if the vision of the Milky Way touched him as it always touched me.

He slowly turned in a circle.

"I've never…"

"You can't in the city. You have to get away from the light to really see the stars."

He shouted in glee, "A shooting star."

"You stand here long enough, you'll see hundreds."

I moved closer to him and put my hand on his shoulder and pointed.

"See the star that's slowly moving. It's a satellite or maybe the space station."

"No way."

"Maybe it's the satellite for your game."

He laughed. I stepped back. He continued turning. He raised his arms. "Look! The whole sky is filled with stars. I can't believe it. There must be hundreds of thousands."

"Millions. And these are just the one we can see."

"Do you know the constellations?"

"No, I've never learned. I don't want to see the part. I want to see the whole."

He nodded and I wondered if he understood.

He kept slowly turning. "It's amazing. It's absolutely amazing. I can't believe it. The stars have always been there, but I've never really seen them."

"Not everyone does. You have to learn how to look."

I swept my hand up to the sky. "Remember this, Colin. This is why we live because life gives us moments like this."

I backed away and stood. I watched the boy bathed in starlight gaze to the sky.

CHAPTER 44

The boy walked slowly up and down the sandbar. Each change of position brought him a new view of the firmament. I let him be. My knee ached. I went and sat on my kayak.

It wasn't my dad who brought me here, but Mia. She was always one for the stars, but the view from our dock was never enough for her. She said we had to get away from shore and the trees. We needed to go out on the lake where we could have a panoramic view of the horizon.

She led me here. So many times we would walk up and down this sandbar. When she had her fill of the stars, she would start to talk and I would join her. The sandbar was not the place to talk about the nuances of everyday living. In the starlight, we would share our hopes and dreams, our fears and longings. The sandbar became our confessional. We had reached the point in our friendship where we had complete trust in one another. We revealed our most intimate thoughts. We exposed our souls and tried to accept our frailties and to strengthen each other.

In many of my talks with Mia we would go back to our youth. We'd talk about the mistakes that we made; the pain that we caused and the pain inflicted upon us. Adults carry the scars of childhood. I looked at the boy and thought: If you can just survive your youth the scars will heal with time.

I must have drifted away again. The boy stood in front of me. The sky had lightened in the east behind him and the stars had faded.

I asked, "Are you ready to go?"

"I'm hungry."

I smiled. I tried to push up off the kayak, but slipped back. My knee had stiffened. I reached for my paddle and used it like a staff. My leg quivered as I tried to stand. The boy took my free arm and he pulled. I stood. I let the boy help me into the kayak. When I was settled, he pushed my kayak from the sandbar.

We paddled side by side. Mist hung over the water. The sun rose and chased the stars away.

CHAPTER 45

We returned to the cottage. I made pancakes. The boy smothered them with butter and syrup, but I didn't mind. I took my ibuprofen with a sip of coffee and then sat with the boy. I propped my left leg up on a chair to try and bring down the knee's swelling.

I asked, "Are you having a good time?"

"I am."

"You act surprised."

The boy smiled. "I am."

I laughed.

"What will you do when I leave? You'll be all alone."

"I have my books and my memories."

He asked with concern, "But you won't have a friend."

"But I do."

"Who?"

"Mia."

Colin stopped cutting his pancakes. He stared at me.

"I think about her all the time." I lowered my voice and turned from his gaze. "I still talk to her."

"Does she talk to you?" I looked to the boy to see if he was making fun of me, but he was serious.

"When you get to know someone so completely, you know how they think. I know what Mia would say."

I pictured her sitting with us. She would so enjoy this breakfast.

The sadness came upon me. I don't know if I said to myself or to the boy, "I have my memories, but how I wish she was still here."

I sat. If only I could reach out and hold her hand and see her smile.

"Are you OK?" His young voice was timid.

I would have plenty of time to mourn later. Right now, I had the boy.

I tried to lighten my voice, "I'm fine. Finish your pancakes. They're getting cold."

I slid my leg off the chair and went to get another cup of coffee.

CHAPTER 46

I went out to the porch to read. The boy stayed at the kitchen table with his iPad.

I must have dozed off. A distant rumble of thunder woke me. It took a while to get my bearings. The sky was full of swirling dark clouds. Waves lashed angrily against the shore. A sudden jolt of fear shook me. I thought maybe the boy had taken out Mia's kayak. I quickly walked to the screen and looked to the dock. I released a breath when I saw the two kayaks.

I checked the cottage. The boy was still at the kitchen table. His head rested on his arms. Drool caked the corner of his mouth. The sight brought me back to high school and boys falling asleep at their desks during study hour. The iPad was silent. I wondered if it too went into sleep mode.

I quietly got a glass from the cupboard and filled it with juice from the refrigerator. The photo albums were still stacked at the end of the table. I set the juice down and took up our Paris photo album. The boy had seen the photos. It was time to put it away. I carried it to the bookcase in the living room.

One photo album had been left on the bookcase. I put the Paris album down and picked it up. It was the photos from Jackie's wedding.

I opened the book and held it in one hand. I glanced through the photos. I could see the father in the boy. He was a handsome man, tall with a ready smile. I understood love and the power it held over a man. What I couldn't understand was how a man could abandon his child.

The wooden floorboard creaked. The boy stood in the kitchen doorway. He rubbed his eyes and stared at me.

"You have more pictures?" He ambled across the room with a teenager's loose gait.

I held my hand up to stop him. "Let's go sit at the table."

"Let me pee." He walked to the bathroom.

I worried about how the boy would react. I didn't know if this was the right time, but is there ever a right time? I took the book and sat at the table.

The boy came from the bathroom. He pulled a chair over and sat beside me. I kept my hands on the closed album.

I studied his face as I said, "These are the pictures of your mom's wedding."

There was a brief look of surprise and then wariness.

"I've never seen them. There are no pictures of him in our house."

"Your dad?"

He snapped, "I don't have a dad!"

He pulled the album from my hands and slid it in front of him. He opened the cover. He stared at the classic wedding photo. The bride and groom standing together with their arms wrapped around each other's waist as they smiled at the camera. Jackie was radiant and the groom was handsome.

Like a flash of lightning, he slammed the cover back down. He swept the album from the table. It hit the wall then crashed to the floor. He knocked his chair back and ran from the kitchen. My knee locked as I stood too quickly. I hobbled after the boy.

When I got to the porch he was already by the lake. He pulled Mia's kayak to the water.

I screamed, "Colin, stop!"

He pushed the kayak into the water. Waves rocked the boat as he climbed into the cockpit.

"Colin!"

He wouldn't stop. I used the handrail to hop down the steps. I quickly limped to the dock. The boy was paddling into the approaching storm.

"Colin! Come back!"

The paddle rose and fell as if he was beating the water.

CHAPTER 47

Wind makes waves; the stronger the wind, the rougher the waves. The boy fought against the dominating forces of wind and waves that tried to push the kayak back to shore.

I stood at the end of the dock and shouted, "Colin!"

If it was a calm day, his frantic paddling would have taken him far out into the lake, but the waves kept pushing him back. He was close to Mia's resting place.

The sky had darkened with whirling gray clouds. Lightning flashed on the horizon and thunder rumbled. The boy didn't know how to handle the kayak in a storm. You had to keep the bow pointed into the surging waves.

A sudden gust of wind caught the bow of the boat and pushed the kayak sideways. The boy couldn't compensate in time. The next wave caught the kayak broadside. Colin was caught with his paddle out of the water. One second he was there and the next he was gone.

The kayak capsized. The paddle was jarred from the boy's hands as it hit the water. I didn't think. I dived into the lake.

I knew I couldn't fight the waves to get to him. I swam underwater. I swam until I thought my lungs would burst. I surfaced. Waves slapped my face. The bottom of the rocking boat wasn't much farther. The boy struggled to get out of the kayak, but the force of the surging, tumbling water kept him pinned in the boat. His head was barely above water. Another wave hit and he disappeared. There was no time. I had to get to the boy.

I slipped beneath the waves and swam with my heart pounding in my ears. There was a dark shape in front of me. It had to be the boy and the kayak. I swan. The boy's face was frantic as he struggled. Each time he tried to escape, the kayak would violently thrash and a new wave would pin him.

I finally got to the boat. The boy saw me. He tried to grab me. There was no time to try and free him. I swam behind the boy and surfaced. The kayak slammed into me. I grabbed hold of the bottom of the kayak and held on. I stretched and reached for the far side. I grabbed the edge. I didn't have the strength to flip the boat. I had to let my weight and the waves and the wind do the work for me. I pulled and slid back. The waves and wind caught and righted the boat. The next moment Mia's kayak was on top of me. I was pinned under the boat.

I knew I had to let go of the kayak. I had to let it pass over me. I pushed away. The waves rocked the boat past me. I broke to the surface gasping. I quickly grabbed the edge of the cockpit and held on. Lightning flashed and a torrent of rain fell from the sky. The boy was hunched over the cockpit. I didn't know if he was dead or alive. He retched. It was the most beautiful sound.

I held on.

I was on the windward side of the kayak. My body was like an anchor. The boat wouldn't capsize as long as I held on. The wind and waves were now our friends. They were pushing us home.

My chest hurt. My heart wasn't right. It was fluttering and it felt for a while that it would stop and then race. I tried to breathe deep to bring it back into rhythm.

The boy put his hand on top of mine. He leaned over me in the pouring rain and said, "She told me I would be OK."

"Who?"

"Grandma. She told me you were coming for me."

I didn't know what to say. I turned and looked to Mia's resting place.

CHAPTER 48

I let the waves do most of the work. I held onto the boat. My feet touched the soggy bottom. I turned the kayak so that the bow was pointed toward shore. I tried to walk through the seaweed. I felt dizzy and wobbly. My heart just wouldn't settle. Waves pushed me and the kayak up on the beach next to our dock.

The boy revived as only the young can. He climbed out of the kayak.

He shouted, "The paddle."

Waves had pushed Mia's paddle toward the dock. The boy forced his legs through the heavy surf and retrieved it.

I tried to drag Mia's kayak up on the beach, but I couldn't. My legs quivered and then buckled. I fell to the pebbly sand. I sat in the shallow water with my hands resting on my knees. My head spun. I was so dizzy that I felt sick. I leaned forward and lowered my head between my knees. The rain poured. Lightning had passed, but I still heard thunder.

"Grandpa."

The voice was next to me.

I tried to say, "Just give me a minute," but I don't know if the boy heard me.

I don't know what was scarier, the feeling in my chest or the dizziness. I put my index fingers on the side of my face in front of the openings for my ears. I pushed hard and then released. I felt my ears pop. The dizziness cleared.

I sat with the waves pounding against me in the shallow surf. I tried to settle my breathing. It felt like hours, but I knew it was only long moments or perhaps a few minutes until my heart settled into its normal rhythm. The boy stood over me with his body blocking the rain.

I lifted my hand. "Help me up."

The boy reached under my armpit and pulled me up with a strength that surprised me.

I stood for a moment to see if the dizziness and arrhythmia would return. The boy held onto my arm.

I drew a deep breath and said, "Let's get out of the rain."

The boy helped me to the cottage.

It was dark from the storm and the encroaching night. I walked up on the porch. I turned on the light and collapsed on my chair. My wet clothes soaked the chair, but I didn't care.

I studied the boy. It was my turn to ask, "Are you OK?"

He lifted his hands palms up by his chest and closed and opened his fingers. He drew a deep breath. His chest expanded. He exhaled.

"Everything seems to be working. I guess I'm OK."

I motioned him closer. I took his hand. It felt cold and clammy. I looked at his nails. They were pink, which was good. I looked at his face. It was pale, but his lips were red.

"Take another deep breath for me."

I listened intently. I heard no rasping or wheezing. I clasped his hand with both of mine. I sat and thought how close I came to losing him.

The boy must have felt my fear. He looked so contrite as he said, "I'm sorry." He sank to his knees in front of my chair. "I don't know what got into me."

I lifted and curled my hand around his cheek. "Everyone make mistakes, Colin. That's part of growing, but you have to learn to stop and think. There are some mistakes you can't survive. Life doesn't give everyone a second chance."

I hoped my words would touch and change him.

The boy nodded. I slipped my hand down and squeezed his shoulder.

"I need a hot chocolate. I think you could use one too."

His whole face changed as he smiled. He stood. He held out his hand to help me up.

CHAPTER 49

I slid out of my clothes and put on my robe. The boy changed clothes as I made the hot chocolate. We sat at the kitchen table. The drinks warmed us. The adrenaline rush passed. The boy seemed to sink into his chair.

"Tired?" I asked.

He nodded.

"But you're OK?"

He lifted his cup and nodded again.

He seemed fine, but I worried. When I was a youngster, a boy had almost drowned in the lake. The toddler thought he could swim. He jumped off the pier and quickly floundered. His older sister ran for help. He was unconscious when his mother pulled him from the water. She used CPR and the boy revived. What seemed like good news didn't last. The boy died of what they called secondary drowning. Water had gotten into his lungs. He died of pneumonia a week later.

I pushed away from the table. "Wait here for a minute."

It didn't take long to find what I was looking for. It was where I thought it would be with Mia's medical things. I brought the small black gadget back to the kitchen.

"Give me your hand."

The boy held his hand out and I clipped the small device to the end of his middle finger.

"What is it?"

"It's an oximeter. It measures the oxygen level in your blood. It'll only take a second."

I turned his hand so that we could both see the digital display.

"It's 96, that's good. Anything over 95 is good."

"I don't understand."

I didn't want to scare him. "It shows how well your lungs are working to get oxygen in your blood. We'll just keep checking it for the next day or two." I added to reassure him. "You're fine."

I unclipped the oximeter and set it on the table.

"I think we both need to get off to bed. It's been a long day."

The boy laughed. "Long day, is that what it was?"

I stood and ruffled his hair. "Off you go."

I tried to read for a while on the porch, but my mind kept reliving the day's events. I gave up and lay on the cot. I tossed and turned. Finally, I went to check on the boy. I waited outside his door and listened. All I heard was silence.

I quietly opened the door. I was met with soft snores. I tiptoed into the room. The boy lay on his side in the glow of the nightlight. His face looked so serene in sleep.

His iPad, the screen now dark, was clutched in his hand. I took it from him and placed it on the night table. He stirred, but didn't waken. I gently touched his forehead. It was cool, no sign of fever. I backed away to the doorway. I left the door open.

I knew I wouldn't hear him from the porch. I walked across the narrow hallway to our bedroom. I sank into the familiar comfort of our bed. The mattress was old and conformed to the contours of my body. I could hear the boy's reassuring snores.

I pulled Mia's pillow close to me. I inhaled her scent. It was reassuring to still sense her essence.

I thought of the boy's words and how he said Mia had talked to him. My rational mind said it couldn't have happened, but I believe in the boy's mind that it did.

CHAPTER 50

Our bedroom windows faced the east. I woke with the sun. The cottage was still. I turned to Mia's side of the bed. Countless days through countless years I had woken with my wife, my love, next to me. I can't describe the loss, the pain that I felt as I reached out and touched the empty space. The pain has never left me.

I sat on the edge of the bed. I was stiff and every muscle seemed to ache. I needed to check on the boy and then I needed to swim.

I stood. I wouldn't leave the bed unmade. I straightened the sheet and blanket. I gently fluffed Mia's pillow and set it in its place.

The boy was deep in slumber. The body heals as it sleeps. I figured the boy would sleep on for hours. I'd leave him to his dreams. I went to swim.

The air is always so fresh and clear the morning after a storm. The sky was cloudless and radiant. It was already warm. I knew the August day would be a scorcher.

I walked to the dock. I slipped on my goggles and climbed down the ladder. The water was calm and warm and soothing. I swam. My muscles relaxed and my mind drifted.

The boy was on the dock when I returned. He sat with his legs dangling over the edge. He wore his cap. I was surprised that he didn't wear a T-shirt. His arms were darkly tanned next to his pale chest. He leaned over toward me as I dog paddled to the ladder.

"I want to take the kayak out."

He must have read the surprise on my face.

"It wasn't the kayak's fault. I'm the one who screwed up."

I climbed the ladder to bide time. I climbed one step at a time. I used my right leg to do the work and let my left leg follow.

The boy pleaded his case. "The sky's clear. There's not a cloud to be seen. I'll keep checking. If it clouds up, I'll come home. I promise."

He sounded confident. I knew I had no choice. I had to let him go. I walked to Mia's kayak. There was some muddy water in the bottom.

"Help me lift it."

We lifted the kayak and stood it on end.

"Hold on to it."

The boy held the kayak up while I ran my hands along the entire bottom. There were some scratches, but nothing deep. When I reached the end, I unscrewed the plug. Water trapped in the kayak rushed out through the drain.

"Shake it a little bit."

The last of the lake water dribbled out. I helped the

boy lower the kayak. Together, we carried it to the lake. He picked up the paddle and straddled the boat.

"Aren't you forgetting something?"

"It's too hot. I don't want to wear a shirt."

"You put on sunblock?"

The boy huffed.

"You'll come back redder than a lobster."

He whined, "Fine."

He dropped the paddle and ran up to the cottage. He came back with his chest lathered with lotion. He handed me the sunblock.

"I can't do my back."

I laughed and spun him around. His skin was soft and smooth and white as a lily.

"You're good. Off you go."

He pushed the kayak into the lake and quickly scrambled in. The boat rocked. He paddled out a ways and then spun in a circle.

Our eyes met. The boy surprised me. He showed not even a hint of fear. Maybe he figured he survived the worst that could happen.

I saluted him. He smiled and saluted me back. He dug the paddle into the water and spun away.

CHAPTER 51

I went and sat on my chair at the lake's edge. Water tickled my ankles. Some days I think the lake is like a woman. She has so many different moods. She got her tantrum out of the way yesterday and today she was in a playful mood.

I watched the boy. He didn't seem in a hurry. He leisurely paddled around the lake as he basked in the sunlight. I felt like he thought the goal was just to have a good time and not to worry about the destination.

I would only have the boy for a few more days and then he would off with his mother to California. I knew he was deeply troubled. Parents don't realize the trauma it causes their children when they separate. Especially in the formative years, teenagers need love and stability. If you shatter the center of their lives, they spin out of control.

The boy not only had the tragic trauma of divorce, but was suffering from the feeling of abandonment. I can't believe that a father would abandon his son and I wondered if he willingly did.

Colin's father left his mother for another woman. I know my daughter. If you hurt her, she will hurt you

back. Filled with righteous anger, Jackie could be mean
and vindictive. I think she has found a way to stop Joe
from seeing his son.

I gazed out at my grandson. The boy is just a pawn. I
think he knows he can't play in his parents' game. Maybe
that's why he hides in another.

CHAPTER 52

I sat reading in the shade of our porch. The air was hot and stagnant. Every so often, I'd glance up and look through the screens to search for the boy. He had been gone for hours, but I wasn't really worried. There was a lot to explore on the lake and then there was the Pointe with the sandbar to stop at and cool off in the water.

I saw the boy. I went and took out two bottles of water from the fridge. I left the shade of the cottage and went into the bright sunshine and sat in my chair by the water to wait.

Tubing seems to be the latest thrill on the lake. It started out with just a simple tire's inner tube. Now all sorts of floats are being towed around the lake by speedboats. Children shriek with laughter as they hang on for dear life as the rafts bounce across the boat's wakes.

Today there are many more tubers than skiers on our lake. In some ways, I think it's a reflection of our times. Skiing takes skill. Tubing is just a matter of holding on.

A powerboat crossed in front of the boy. The tethered raft quickly followed. Two gangling teenagers bounced atop the float as they held on. The wake from the boat and raft rocked Mia's kayak. The boy used his body weight and the paddle to steer the kayak into the wake. He was a fast learner. The kayak smoothly rode over the turbulent waves and then settled into the calm beyond.

Life isn't just about holding on. The boy could learn. Somehow I had to help him.

"You're running out of time."

I glanced at Mia's empty chair. I knew her words were just in my mind, but I also knew that's what she would say.

The boy pulled Mia's kayak up on shore. He slid the paddle inside and then walked toward me. His chest was red. I hated to think what he would look like if he hadn't put on sunblock.

I pointed to his chest. "Does it hurt?"

He glanced down at his stomach. He smiled. He looked as though he thought he was wearing a badge of honor.

"No. Not really."

"It will tonight. I have some aloe lotion you can put on."

He shrugged. I tossed him a water bottle. It bounced off his fingers. He quickly bent and scooped it up as if nothing had happened.

I laughed. "Good hands."

"My hands are wet." He made a show of wiping his hands on his swimsuit.

He walked and then collapsed on Mia's chair next to me.

I don't know when it had happened, but I felt comfortable having him sit by me. I think he felt the same.

I asked, "So, how was it?"

"Great." He pointed to the far end of the lake. "The water's so clear. You can see fish swimming beneath the kayak." He laughed. "I'd spit in the water and they'd come up to the surface. If I had a net, I could have caught 'em."

"How big were they?"

"Well …"

"That's why fishermen leave them alone. You won't get a meal out of them. They'll wait until the fish are big enough to go to out to the deep."

He uncapped his bottle and took a deep swallow.

"I suppose you're hungry?"

"I could eat."

"If you're up to it, we could walk to Walt's Diner."

"Don't you drive anywhere?"

"Not if I can help it."

He laughed. "Can I take a shower first?"

"Good idea."

He bounced up and fast walked up to the cottage.

Mia's chair was empty, but I knew if she was there, she would smile.

CHAPTER 53

We had an early dinner at Walt's Diner. Of course that meant that the few other patrons were about my age. The boy didn't seem to mind being in a room full of old people. He quickly devoured his burger and fries. He slurped his milk shake and asked for another.

"Have you lived here all your life?"

"My dad built the cottage when I was about your age. I've always been able to spend my summers here except for when I was in the Army."

I perked his interest.

"You were in the Army?"

"Just for a couple of years."

"Were you in a war?"

I was going to say that there are some things that I didn't want to talk about, but I couldn't expect the boy to be honest with me if I wasn't honest with him.

"I was in the war in Viet Nam."

His boyish face changed and I think he suddenly saw me in a different light.

"Did you ever kill anyone?"

It was a question an adult wouldn't ask, but it was a

question a teenager would blurt out without thinking.

"No."

He seemed disappointed.

"I was a medic. My job was to try and save people, not kill them."

"That's cool. I bet you were good at it."

I lowered my voice and said, "I don't remember the ones I saved. I only remember the ones I lost."

The memories came and I knew I had to leave them.

"Your grandmother didn't want me to go. It was the biggest argument we ever had. I could have gone to college with her and gotten a deferment. But I didn't think it was right to have some other boy go in my place."

"Were you ever wounded?"

"There are many types of wounds, Colin. Some are visible. You can see the missing arm or the burned face. Everyone who went to Viet Nam was wounded, but for many, the scars are hidden inside."

I pushed the salt and pepper shakers around the table. "I came back to the lake to heal. Your grandmother came and stayed with me."

The boy stayed quiet. It was up to me to fill the silence.

"Mia would hold me when I'd wake from the nightmares. She'd walk me down to the dock and together we would sit and wait for the sunrise."

I glanced at my grandson. "They say time heals all. It doesn't. The memories of Viet Nam are still with me like ghosts in the corner. Mia taught me how to accept the memories. She also taught me how to live in the present and see the beauty around us."

I took a sip from my water glass. "When Mia went back to school in the fall, I went to school with her. I never left her again."

CHAPTER 54

We were quiet on the walk back to the cottage. The talk with the boy stirred too many memories that wouldn't settle. I looked at my grandson as he ambled ahead of me down the well-worn path. I wondered what scars he already carried. I wondered what new scars await him.

He stopped to scoop up and then throw a pebble into the woods. Two squirrels scampered up a tree trunk. They perched on a branch with their bushy tails curled above their backs. They stared at us.

I needed to be honest with the boy. I caught up to him. "It was my choice to make, Colin."

He gave me his quizzical glance.

"Viet Nam. I didn't have to go. Many of my friends dodged the draft by running off to college. Jake got in his car one morning and started driving north. He didn't stop until he reached Canada. He never came back.

"It's true that I didn't want another boy to go in my place. But it's also true that I wanted to experience life. I wanted to be like a Hemingway character. Viet Nam was a chance to challenge myself. To see what I was made of.

"In Viet Nam, I saw the darkest part of man. War changes you. It strips the innocence from your soul. You can never get it back."

I started walking. The boy matched my stride.

"You're going to have so many choices to make in your life, Colin. Choices are like dominoes: each one you make will affect the next."

The boy asked in his serious tone that belied his age, "So, how do I know what's the right choice?"

"No one can answer that question but you. You have to think it through. You have to stop and listen to your feelings. You need to decide what's best for you and when you decide, you have to be willing to live with your choices."

CHAPTER 55

The boy went into the cottage to be reunited with his iPad. I went and sat on my chair by the lake.

Colin shouted from the screen door, "The red light's blinking on your phone."

I shouted back, "It's probably just another robocall."

I had just gotten settled. I didn't want to get up again. I tried to remember if I had checked the machine today. I couldn't remember. I reluctantly pushed up and walked to the cottage.

The boy sat at the kitchen table. He played his game.

Without looking up he asked, "Why don't you have a cell phone?"

"I don't want to be bothered."

He shrugged and continued his game.

There were six messages on the answering machine. It didn't matter that I was on a do-not-call list. The robocalls kept coming. I'd listen to the first three words – by then I could tell if it was a recording. If it was, I'd hit the delete button and go to the next message. One call was from the pharmacy about my meds. I had enough to last until the boy left. I would pick them up next week.

I played the last message. Jackie's high-pitched voice filled the room.

"Hi Dad…" She paused as if she was thinking of what to say next. I could picture her twirling her hair around her finger. "I guess you guys are out. We're having a great time. I can't believe it's over so soon. We leave tomorrow and with the layovers, I won't get to Detroit until Sunday morning. I'll rent a car and come and pick up Colin. Can you make sure that he's ready? We're booked on a flight back to California later in the afternoon. I have to be back to work on Monday morning. Um …" I could hear a voice in the background. "I've got to run. We have reservations for dinner. Love you guys. Make sure Colin's ready."

I shook my head and thought my daughter will never change.

I asked, "What day is it?"

The boy looked pale. He worried his lower lip just like his mother did.

"It's Friday."

Suddenly, I felt so sad for the boy. He seemed so distraught. I know life with his mother isn't easy. And then there's all the trauma of going to a new high school and trying to fit in. He doesn't have his father to help him and to be a foil against Jackie.

I wondered what Jackie's boyfriend was like. Did he want a family with an already made son? How would the boy react to him? There were too many questions with no answers. He sat with a helpless plea on his face.

I could keep him with me, but that was just the wishing of a lonely old man. I don't know how many morning swims I have left. If something happened to me the boy would be stranded and all alone. There is really no choice: the boy would have to go with his mother.

The whole time I'm thinking, he's watching me. No matter what my heart wanted, I would have to send him away. He must have read the answer on my face. He crushed me with his look of betrayal. He picked up his iPad and walked to his bedroom.

CHAPTER 56

I went down to the lake and sat in my chair. I reached out and touched the empty armrest of Mia's chair next to mine. How I wished I could just hold her hand. She would know what to do. She always did. I thought and I thought, but I had no answer for the boy.

I walked to the dock. The sky above the lake was crystalline. It would be a glorious sunset. I needed to get the boy.

The cottage was silent. I quietly walked to the closed bedroom door. There were no beeps from the game. I wondered if the boy had fallen asleep. I gently rapped my knuckles against the door.

"Colin."

My voice was met with silence. I opened the door. The boy turned on the bed away from me. I walked into the room and sat on the edge of the bed. I rested my hand on his shoulder. We sat in the quiet of the moment.

I squeezed his shoulder. The boy lifted and rested his hand on top of mine. He sighed. It was a sigh that could break a man's heart. I gently pulled him over onto his back. His eyes were red and puffy. He seemed lost. A teenager is just a grown boy with a child's heart.

I tried to put some lightness into my voice. "Come on. I want you to see something." I gave his shoulder a reassuring squeeze. "I'll wait for you outside."

I pushed up from the bed. My knees creaked as I stood. I left the boy to follow when he was ready.

I stood and waited on the dock. It wasn't long until I heard the screen door slam. I turned and waved the boy to me. He had put his cap on and it looked like he had washed his face. I smiled. He returned a small upward tilt of his lips.

He asked, "Where're we going?"

"We're already there."

I bent and put my hand down on the dock. I used my palm for balance as I lowered my body and sat on the edge of the wooden slats. I dangled my legs over the side. The boy plopped down next to me.

"What are we doing?"

"We're not doing anything. We're just going to enjoy the sunset."

The boy did his shoulder shrug. He stared out at the water. I wanted to talk, but I knew it wasn't the right time. I gazed at him out of the corner of my eye. He slumped a little as his body relaxed. His breathing slowed.

The Jet Skis and tubers had left the lake. Pontoon boats slowly floated across the calm water for their sunset cruises. It was the time of the evening that stillness descended upon us. Birds flew overhead as they darted to their nighttime nests.

The sky changed. It was a subtle change of colors. The bright afternoon hues darkened. White puffy clouds turned gray. Pink rays turned purple as they streaked across the heavens.

The sun would set behind the trees across the lake. Full branches swayed. The leaves were green with a touch of brownish yellow. Fall was coming.

A flock of geese honked as they flew south overhead. The boy followed their path. A mother from one of the lake cottages called her children home. Below our feet, a turtle popped his head above the water. He took a look at us and then dove beneath the surface.

Time passed. We sat in silence. The sun sank behind the trees. Twilight came. Tree trunks threw their lengthening shadows across the water.

The boy raised his legs up to his chest and wrapped his arms around them. He rested his chin on his knees. His blue eyes gazed upon our lake.

I wondered what he was thinking.

CHAPTER 57

The sun set. I turned and looked behind me. There was just a glimmer of stars on the far horizon. In the twilight, the boy sat immobile as a statue with his hands clasped around his knees. He seemed hypnotized by the sunset.

"Colin."

He turned his head to me and rested his cheek on his knee.

"I wish I had the answers for you, but I don't. Life is hard sometimes."

He laughed. "It sucks."

I nodded my head in agreement. "Sometimes it does, but not always. I've lived a long time." I pointed my hand to the horizon. "I've seen such beauty. I've known the love of a woman who will never leave me. But there are also times when life is filled with pain. We're human. I've made my share of mistakes and I suffered greatly from the mistakes of others. No one should have a young man die in his arms."

The boy stared at me. He lost his youthful curious demeanor. Now he seemed grave.

I swallowed and drew a breath. I had so much I wanted to say to the boy. I searched for the right words.

"When I came back from Viet Nam, I didn't know how to go on living. I carried the dead and the maimed home with me. I couldn't let them go. Mia taught me that I didn't have to let them go, but I would have to find a way to go on living with them.

"What she taught me was that I was the only one who could save me. I was the only person who could make my life better. There is strength inside us, Colin. It's part of our nature, our need to survive. It took me a long time to find the strength I needed to survive. It was a long time until the day came when I could smile at Mia.

"I don't know what happened between your mother and father. They're adults. It's not my business. My concern is for you. I know how hard your parents have made your life, but you are not the only teenager who suffers. There are many who face far greater wounds then you.

"What I have learned in life, Colin, is that you are the only person who can make your life better. You have to find your strength. You are the only one who can heal your wounds.

"Life is hard right now, but I promise it will get better. There is so much joy in life waiting for you. There are friends to be made and laughs to be shared. There is a kiss out there that will capture your heart. There our children to hold and rock to sleep at night. An old wrinkled hand to caress in the sunset. But these joys won't come to you if you're hiding in a game."

The boy sat still. I couldn't read his face. I didn't know what else I could say.

I turned away from him. I lifted my legs and rolled onto my knees. I pulled one knee up to my chest and used my hand to try and push up from the dock. The boy quickly stood. He leaned over me and put his hand under my armpit. My knee creaked in protest as he helped me to my feet. We faced each other. A mosquito landed on his cheek. I brushed it away.

"The squitos are coming. We'd best get inside."

I took a step. My knee locked. I grimaced as I hobbled another step. The boy came to my side. He lifted my hand and slid under my arm. I let my weight rest on his shoulder.

We walked to the cottage.

CHAPTER 58

Mist was like a delicate veil floating above our tranquil lake. I took one step at a time down the dock's ladder and slid into the water. I treaded for a while to let my knee loosen. I pulled down my goggles and began my swim. It took a while for my heart and body to fall in rhythm. It took even longer to let my mind wander.

As I swam, my thoughts kept returning to the boy. This was our last full day together. He hadn't left, but already I missed him.

I swam to my halfway point, the train trestle. Sunlight reflected off the rusty steel. I turned for my homeward stretch. I did my backstroke for a time. I stayed close to shore and listened for boats.

The mist was gone when I finished my swim. I treaded water in front of our cottage. I was between Mia and the dock. I scanned the lake. It was still too early for Jet Skis and tubers. I went to find my wife.

I checked my marker points on shore. I knew I was in the right spot. I hyperventilated and slid beneath the calm. I swam to the bottom. I squeezed my nose and forced air to into my nostrils to equalize the building pressure in my ears. I reached the seaweed and searched for Mia. I stayed for as long as I could. I didn't find her. I kicked to the surface. I gulped a breath. I lifted my legs and floated on my back. My heart pounded. I waited for the flutter, but it didn't come. My heart and breathing slowed. I drifted.

I realized there was no reason to continue my search. Mia had her wish granted. She was part of the water around me. The sun touched my face and the warm water soothed me.

CHAPTER 59

I sat on my chair by the lake's edge. The bright sun dried my skin. I heard the screen door shut and then footsteps on the path behind me.

The boy appeared and sat in Mia's chair. He stretched his legs out and his arms up over his head. His hair was still tousled from sleep.

He asked, "How was your swim?"

"It was good. There's no such thing as a bad swim."

"Why do you do it? I mean, every morning you're out there. Doesn't it get boring?"

I stared at our lake. "I've always enjoyed the water. When I came back from Viet Nam, I started swimming. It was therapy. Swimming gave me a chance to escape, to let my mind and body flow with the water. I didn't have to think. I just swam. Each day I would go a little farther until finally the day came when I could swim all the way across the lake. I'd walk the path on the far side of the lake back to the cottage. It went through the woods. I think the exercise helped heal me."

I turned to the boy. "I've always believed in the old adage that a healthy body creates a healthy mind." I smiled at Colin. "You should try it."

He laughed. "But you don't swim across the lake anymore."

My mood changed. I turned away from the boy to the water. I couldn't keep the sadness from creeping into my voice. "Back then it was different. The lake's not safe to swim across now. Not with the Jet Skis and the tubers. It's too dangerous. That's why I have to stay close to shore."

As if to reinforce my words, there came a sudden high-pitched growing whine. Two Jet Skis zigzagged across the water as they raced upon the lake.

I waited until they passed. "At one time our lake was a sanctuary. Now … I don't know what it has become."

I shook off the mood. It was the boy's last day. I'd have plenty of time to grieve later.

"So what do you want to do today?"

The boy raised his eyebrows and tapped his fingers on the armrest. "I don't know. I thought maybe we could just hang here today." He gazed at the clear light blue sky. "Maybe I could take the kayak out and go to the Pointe?"

"Sounds like a plan. Why don't you do that? I'll go to Churchill's and pick up some food for dinner."

"Your one and only chicken and rice?"

"You don't like it?'

The boy laughed. "It's not bad."

"I can get you some macaroni and cheese."

He shook his head. "No. I'll get plenty of that at home. Let's do chicken and rice." He looked to the pit. "Can we have a fire tonight?"

"I don't see why not. We can roast s'mores."

" S'mores?"

"You'll like them."

We exchanged a comfortable smile.

I reached over and tapped his knee. "I'm going to head in and take a shower. You be careful out there."

"I'll keep an eye on the sky."

CHAPTER 60

The cottage was quiet when I returned from Churchill's. I realized that soon it would be quiet for a long time. Sadness came with the thought of solitude. I put the food away. I walked out to the porch. Mia's kayak was gone. There was no sign of the boy.

I sat in my chair and picked up Hemingway. I had finished *A Moveable Feast* and moved on to *The Old Man and the Sea*. I don't know how many times I had read the book, but I always found something new. I loved Hemingway's description of the sea. I was at the point in my life where I understood the loneliness of the old man.

I dozed off. The book falling to the floor woke me. I bent and picked it up. I looked outside and tried to gauge the time. It must be late afternoon. My naps were getting longer.

I set the book to the side and pushed up. I stood for a few seconds to let the blood rush back to my head. I walked to the screen. My kayak was in its spot, but Mia's kayak was still gone. I searched the lake, but there was no sign of the boy. A few clouds had rolled in, but they were white and puffy, not the bringers of storms.

The boy would be hungry when he came home. It was time to start dinner.

I kept expecting to hear the screen door slam and the boy's footsteps. Minutes passed slowly. The chicken and rice were done. I turned off the stove. I covered the pan and let the food cool on top of the stove. I walked out to the porch and down to the lake.

I stood on the dock. It was Saturday and even though it was dinnertime, the weekenders were out in force. The lake was buzzing with Jet Skis and tubers. The interlopers knew fall was approaching and come Labor Day their season would be over.

I paced the dock. I don't know why I was worried, but I was.

I sat in my chair. I didn't know where the boy was. Long minutes passed as fear gnawed my stomach. I kept telling myself the boy was fine. That he just lost track of time as boys do. Any second, I expected Mia's kayak to round the bend and then I would be able to breathe again.

The sun was sinking to the horizon. Jet Skis and tubers gradually disappeared from the lake as evening quickly approached. It would be another glorious sunset.

I knew where the boy was.

CHAPTER 61

I thought to hell with the pain. I quickly walked to my kayak. I picked up the paddle and pushed the boat into the water. The kayak rocked as I struggled into the cockpit. My knee screamed in protest. I dug the paddle into the water and went to stop the boy.

I had to find the right pace. I wanted to get to the boy as fast as I could, but I didn't want to send my heart fluttering. Like when I swam, I needed my heart to fall into the rhythm to match my strong, steady strokes. The kayak glided across the still water.

The lowering sun cast my shadow on the water. I rounded the bend. Sunlight reflected off the train trestle. I squinted. I couldn't see the boy on the bridge. Maybe I was wrong, but I just knew he had to be here. I searched the landing beneath the trestle. Mia's kayak sat abandoned on the sand. I paddled faster.

I kept my eyes on the top of the bridge as I paddled. The boy walked out of the woods to the outside edge of the trestle. He cautiously stepped from one railroad tie to the next. He focused on his feet. He didn't see me approaching beneath him on the lake. I wanted to scream at Colin, to tell him to stop and go back. But I was afraid I would startle the boy and he would lose his balance.

The boy took a few steps, then stopped. He looked across the bridge to mark his progress. He hesitantly took a few more steps. His cap shaded his eyes. I was still too far away to see his face.

I watched his slow progress along the trestle. He stopped. He looked forward and then turned and looked back. He was at the halfway point of the bridge. He inched his feet to the trestle's edge.

I felt like time stopped. Like the moment was the part of a nightmare where I should wake up, but it wasn't a dream.

The boy held his hands out as if testing the air. I was close enough now to see his face. I saw fear but also determination. His legs trembled. I lifted the paddle and set it on top of the kayak. The boat sat still in the water.

The boy looked to the sunset across the lake. He saw me below him. Our eyes met. He smiled. He drew a deep breath.

He jumped.

I felt my heart stop.

CHAPTER 62

The boy hit the water with his knees slightly bent up toward his chest. I quickly paddled to the spot where he disappeared. It was only a few seconds until his head bobbed to the surface, but the seconds seemed to stretch on forever.

He shook his head. Water beads flew from his hair. He treaded water. He raised his arm and shook his fist up at the bridge and screamed, "Yesss!"

I paddled to him. He grabbed the edge of my kayak. His face glowed with triumph.

He shouted, "I did it!"

I didn't know how to answer. I was angry. It was a foolhardy thing to do. But I was also proud of him.

"You did."

He laughed. "I'm glad I'm in the water because I think I peed my pants on the way down."

"It happens."

He looked up at the bridge. "How far up is it?"

The bridge always seems higher to a child.

"I don't know, but it's quite a way."

The boy was exuberant. His mood was contagious.

There would be time to talk later, but for now I needed to let him enjoy the moment.

He felt the top of his head.

I pointed. "Over there."

He swam and retrieved his cap and then came back and held onto the front of the kayak. I paddled to shore. When he was close enough, he walked up on the beach. He stood and stared at the towering trestle above him. He turned to me with 'I can't believe I did it' look on his face. He bent and retrieved Mia's kayak. He pushed it into the water. He glided up next to me.

"Are you hungry?"

He laughed. "I'm starving."

"Let's go home."

We swung our kayaks around and paddled together across our lake into the sunset. Every so often, the boy would turn to look back at the trestle and then smile at me.

CHAPTER 63

I should have bought more chicken. The boy was ravenous. I scraped the bottom of the pan and gave him the last of the rice.

The boy ate every bit. He looked at his empty bowl and then at me.

"We'll have s'mores later."

He pushed back from the table and stretched his legs. He rested his hands on his stomach and sighed contently. I took his bowl and silverware. He gave me another surprise. He stood and helped me clear the table.

"Why don't you put some bug spray on and walk down by the lake. It'll do you some good. Help you walk off your full stomach. I'll do the dishes."

"I can help."

"No, I'm good. It's always been my job. Mia would cook and I would do the dishes. Go. Take a walk. When I'm done, I'll come out and you can help me with the fire."

He shrugged. He turned and left me to my chore. I filled the sink with dish soap and water. It wasn't long until I heard the screen door slam. I looked over my shoulder and saw him skip down the stairs into the night air.

I washed and stacked the dishes. I would let the air dry them. I walked to the table and pushed in the boy's chair. His iPad sat silent on the edge of the table.

I walked down to the lake. There was a touch of coolness in the air that was the harbinger of fall.

I sat on my chair. Frogs and crickets serenaded me. The boy was on the dock. He was illuminated by the lights coming from the cottage behind us. He had gathered a bucket of pebbles. He tried to skip the stones across the top of the calm, starlit water. He threw the stones side-armed. A few would bounce, but most hit and then plummeted to the bottom.

A pontoon boat slowly cruised across the lake. The boat's nightlights looked like stars floating atop the water.

I sat and thought how different my life would be tomorrow. The boy would be gone and I would be all alone. I set my hand atop Mia's armrest. If she was here, she would take my hand and all would be well.

Tomorrow night the stars will still shine. Water will lap upon the shore by my feet. But my world will change.

The boy carried the empty bucket back from the dock. He noticed me sitting alone. I lifted my hand from Mia's armrest. He came and sat in her seat.

"Do you miss her?" He asked.

"Always."

The boy stayed silent. I tried to gather myself.

"I have the memories. Life isn't about what you've accomplished. It's about what you remember. My mother told me when I was young, 'You need to build your memories.' She was right."

The boy asked, "Is that where you go?"

"What do you mean?"

"When you get quiet it seems like you're not really here."

"Perhaps, I don't really know. We shared so much together. Wherever I look, I see my Mia. We were one of the lucky few. We were meant to be together and we stayed together. Do you know how rare that is today? To find a love that lasts a lifetime. I don't know why, but we were blessed."

CHAPTER 64

There is something about building a fire that takes me back to my roots. I'm sure my ancestors in Ireland, before they fled during the time of the Great Hunger, would gather around the fire. They'd share the light and warmth of the hearth and tell their stories.

We sat on our tree stumps across from each other. Flames flickered and danced between us. Smoke drifted to the starlit sky.

I asked, "What made you do it?"

The boy shrugged. He picked up a twig, broke it, and tossed it into the flames.

I waited. I could be patient when I needed to.

The boy had to fill the silence. "I listen to everything that you say." He laughed. "I may not always agree you, but I listen."

He paused. He grew serious and stared at me.

"When you talked about the bridge you said it was a rite of passage. That it was a way to prove to your friends how brave you were. I don't have the childhood that you had. I don't have friends the way that you did."

He picked up another twig and tossed it on the fire. He watched the flames ignite the stick.

"I needed to prove to myself that I could be brave like you."

His answer took me by surprise. I felt guilty. I felt like I had betrayed a scared trust. I didn't want the reminiscing of an old man to put his young life in danger.

"There are many types of bravery, Colin. Sometimes the greatest bravery is just to get up in the morning and somehow make it through the day."

He slowly nodded. I think I finally touched him. Somehow we had bridged the gap of years between us and shared one of the secrets of life.

CHAPTER 65

I always thought making s'mores was easy until the boy tried to make one. His first attempt at roasting marshmallows was a disaster. He kept them at the fire too long. They were blackened and covered with ash. On the second try, he burnt the tips of his fingers when he tried to slide the gooey marshmallows off the stick. I laughed as he licked his fingers. The third try was the charm. The marshmallows melted on top of the chocolate above the graham cracker.

He brought the s'more to his mouth.

"Better let it cool," I said.

He blew on the s'more like a little kid blowing on a spoonful of his macaroni and cheese. He took a bite. White melted marshmallow stuck to his lips as he smiled.

He got the hang of it. He made a s'more for me and then one more for himself. I had almost forgotten how good they were. It had been such a long time since I had a s'more.

Sitting with the boy made me feel younger. His youth and vitality was contagious. He gave me a contented smile across the fire.

"This is pretty neat," he said. "The fire, the s'mores…"
He looked out to the water bathed in starlight "…and
the lake."

"It is."

"A memory."

I nodded and smiled. "You'll always have it with
you."

"I will."

He settled on his log and stared at the fire. I left him
to his thoughts as I too stared at the fire.

CHAPTER 66

I decided to skip my morning swim. The boy would be gone in the afternoon. I wanted to spend as much time with him as I could before he left. I had enough eggs and mix for pancakes. I wished I had some bacon to cook. I think the boy would like some bacon with his pancakes, but Mia wouldn't have red meat in the house. I could hear her say, "Give him some fruit instead."

The boy must have been restless like me this morning. I didn't have to wake him. I heard the toilet flush and then the water run in the bathroom sink. He stumbled to the table. He sank into the kitchen chair. He was still half asleep. He yawned and stretched.

I set a plate of pancakes in front of him. I took the butter and syrup from the fridge and slid the tub and bottle to him.

He mumbled, "Thanks."

I playfully rubbed my hand through his tousled, bedhead hair. I went back to work. I knew the boy would eat the pancakes faster than I could make them.

The sugary syrup seemed to wake him. He looked at the kitchen clock. He seemed surprised by the time.

He asked, "You didn't swim this morning?"

"I took the day off so that I could spend more time with you."

He nodded and spiked another forkful of pancakes.

"We have the morning. What would you like to do today?"

He pondered the question. He chewed and swallowed some pancakes. Another batch was ready. I slid them on his plate.

He asked, while he buttered and cut the pancakes, "Do you have more albums to look at?"

"A few."

"Do you have any pictures of your mom and dad?"

"Why don't you finish up and then go pack. I'll go look for the album."

I set the white album between us on the table. The edges of the album were worn by countless fingers. The photos were old. They were black and white and brittle. They were covered by a sheet of cellophane that had yellowed with the years. A young man stood on a porch dressed in a uniform.

"That's a photo of my dad, your great-grandfather, when he was in the Army. He was drafted when he was in college. It was a different war, World War II. He was a quiet man. I don't know if the war made him quiet or if that was the way he always was."

The next photo was of a young couple. The young woman wore a flowing white dress. My dad wore a black tuxedo. They stood on the steps of a towering cathedral.

The woman held a bouquet of white flowers. They smiled for the camera. The cellophane had bubbled. I tried to smooth it.

"That's my mother, your great-grandmother."

The boy said with a tone of reverence, "She was beautiful,"

"She was. She was a woman ahead of her time. She went to college. Not many girls did back then. I think in some ways she intimidated my dad. After the war, he never went back to school. Your great-grandmother wasn't a stay-at-home mom. She was a teacher.

"When my dad came back from the war, he got a job in a hardware store. He was a hard worker and learned all the ins and outs of the business. When the owner died, my parents took their savings and got a loan from the bank. They bought the store. My dad worked 80 hours a week to make the store a success. He would have worked Sundays if he could, but back then no stores opened on Sunday.

"My dad may have been quiet, but he was a smart man. He knew times were changing. The big chains were coming in. This was way before Walmart and Home Depot. This was the time of Sears, Montgomery Ward, and True Value. He sold the store at a nice profit. He bought our land on the lake and built this cottage. He loved to fish."

"But you don't."

"I never took to it. I think he was disappointed. I was his only child. I think fishing was something he wanted to share with me."

I looked around the cottage and then out the window to our lake.

"There are a lot of memories here: my parents and Mia, Jackie and her friends and the parties they would have." I looked at the boy. "And now you. When I'm gone, your mom will inherit the cottage. I don't know what she will do with our home."

I gazed around the cottage. I could hear the voices of the past. I stopped my wanderings. I needed to focus on the boy. It was his last day.

"Why don't we take the kayaks out onto the lake?"

The boy smiled and said, "Why not."

CHAPTER 67

I expected it to be rainy and dreary to match the mood of the boy's leaving, but it wasn't. It was a glorious day. The sun was bright with just a few pale puffy clouds on the horizon. There was a slight breeze, which put a nice white cap on top of the water and cooled our skin. The trees were turning. Brownish gold and brownish yellow leaves swayed on the far shore. Maybe Mother Nature summoned her best beauty as a parting gift for the boy.

Colin was at home on the water. He had learned how to shift his body to help control the boat's motion. Now, Mia's kayak seemed to be an extension of him.

In just the past two weeks, he had changed. He hadn't lost any pounds, but he repositioned his weight. I could see muscles in his naked shoulders and arms. He darted ahead of me like a young pony yearning to run.

I leisurely paddled. I was happy to follow and watch my grandson.

He led me to the far shore. The water was clear and it was only a few feet to the sandy bottom. He had his fish. They swam beneath his kayak. He leaned and dangled his hand over the water. He wiggled his fingers. Small fish swam around and through the shadow his hand cast on the water.

He smiled at me. I couldn't help but to smile back.

It's easy to lose track of time on the lake. I don't wear a watch, but I knew from the sun that it had to be close to noon.

I looked across the lake to our cottage. A lone figure stood on the dock. We were too far away to see who it was, but I knew it had to be his mother who had come to take him away.

CHAPTER 68

I felt like I was the one who now had to take the lead. We paddled home to the cottage. I set a strong pace. The boy stayed by my side.

My daughter paced the dock with her arms held tight against her chest. I expected to hear her screams across the water, but she held her tongue.

The boy was the first to shore. He quickly got out of his kayak. He came back and helped me get out of my boat.

Jackie came charging down from the dock.

I held my hand up to stop my daughter before she got started. "He's packed and ready to go." I turned to the boy. "Colin, go change out of your swimsuit and gather your things. Better be quick about it."

The boy cast a quick glance at his mother and then ran off to the cottage.

I pulled my kayak up on shore and slid the paddle inside. I had learned the secret to my daughter was to disarm and distract her.

"How was your trip?"

She glanced at her Fitbit to check the time. She

breathed. Her shoulders sagged and she seemed to relax. I don't know if she realized that she smiled.

"We had a lovely time together."

"I'm glad."

"And you and Colin?"

"I think he had a good time. Would you like a cup of coffee? We could sit and talk."

"I'd like to Dad, but there's no time. The flight from Paris was delayed. I'm going to have to run to catch the flight home."

I nodded. It was so like my daughter. Somehow, she always created a whirlwind around her.

I said, "Let's go get the boy."

CHAPTER 70

We walked to the cottage. The boy came out of the screened porch and then down the wooden steps. He wore the outfit he had worn from California, his cargo shorts and T-shirt. He added the Mud Hens cap to his attire. That made me happy.

He carried his backpack by the strap. I could see the top of his iPad in the front pocket. He wouldn't meet my gaze. He looked so sad. That made me even sadder. He started to go around the cottage to the rental car parked out front.

I heard Mia say, "You can't let him leave like this. Go to him."

I called, "Colin."

He stopped. I walked to him. He stared down at his shoes. I touched his chin and turned his face up to me. Our eyes met. The bond was there. I took him into my arms. I cradled his head against my chest.

"You're a good kid and I love you."

He dropped the backpack. He hugged me so hard that it hurt my heart.

"I love you, Grandpa."

Sometimes you just need to hear the words.

I didn't want to let him go, but I knew that I had to. I gently pushed him away.

"Do they have a rowing club at that school you're going to?"

He wiped tears from his cheeks. "I don't know. They might."

"You should check it out. You would be good at it. It would be a good place to meet people and make friends."

He brightened and said, "You don't give up do you?"

"I haven't yet."

I turned so that we could both see the lake.

"It's beautiful here in the fall. The summer people are gone and the lake is so quiet and tranquil. The leaves, the colors, you paddle by the shore and the leaves float down upon you."

I looked upon my grandson. "Maybe you could come for a weekend? I could send you a ticket."

The boy sniffled and then swiped the back of his hand under his nose.

"I'll come."

It was one of the few times in my life where my daughter was speechless. I walked to her and rested my hands on her shoulders.

"Be good to the boy. He needs your love, not your anger."

I saw the chastised child still inside her. I hugged her and she hugged me back.

"You best be off. You have a flight to catch."

I walked to the boy. He bent and picked up his backpack.

Jackie said, "Wait. I want a picture." She opened her purse and took out her cell phone.

"Can we take it by the lake?" The boy asked.

"Why not?"

We walked down by our chairs. We turned back to the cottage. I put my arm around my grandson's shoulder. My other hand rested atop Mia's empty chair. Colin circled his arm around the back of my waist. Jackie lifted her cell phone.

It was easy to smile because the boy gave me hope.

CHAPTER 71

It was dark. I wasn't sure where I was. It was still and quiet. I slowly realized that I was sitting on my chair on the porch. I must have dozed off again. I lifted the book from my lap and set it on the end table. I wondered how long I slept. The cottage felt empty. I knew I was alone.

I left the light off and stood in the dark. My left knee throbbed. I walked to the screen door. The moon glowed on the lake. I opened the door and hobbled down the stairs to the well-worn path.

Mia stood on the dock in the moonlight. I held my breath and walked toward her. She gave me the smile that had captured my heart. She turned and gracefully dived into the water.

I went to her. I reached the end of the dock and searched for my Mia, but all I found were the ripples she left behind.

I followed the ripples across the lake. I saw the boy. He stood on the sandbar gazing up at the stars with wonder.

CHAPTER 72

Colin sat next to his mother. The jet engines hummed. The plane was full and the boy was stiff from sitting still for so long. The cabin lights were dimmed. Like many of the other travelers, his mother had fallen asleep.

He turned off his game. His mother's purse was under the seat in front of her. He bent and took out her cell phone. He went to Google photos and opened the picture of him and his grandfather and the lake.

He imagined what it would be like to be at the lake in the fall with Grandpa.

"Did you have a good time?"

He turned to his mother. "I thought you were asleep."

His mother gently put her hand above his hand holding the cell phone.

He wanted to tell her about the heart-stopping thrill of jumping off the train trestle, but he didn't think she would understand.

He stared at the photo and said, "I did."

Made in the USA
Middletown, DE
24 February 2019